Adapted by Jasmine Jones

Based on the television series, "Lizzie McGuire", created by Terri Minsky

Part One is based on a teleplay written by Melissa Gould

Part Two is based on a teleplay written by Nina G. Bargiel & Jeremy J. Bargiel

New York

Printed in the United States of America

First Edition
3 5 7 9 10 8 6 4

Library of Congress Catalog Card Number: 2002093175

ISBN 0-7868-4543-0
For more Disney Press fun, visit www.disneybooks.com
Visit DisneyChannel.com

Lizzie McGuire

PART ONE

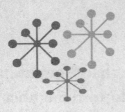

CHAPTER ONE

"Lizzie, there's something I was supposed to tell you," David "Gordo" Gordon said into the phone. "I just can't remember what."

Lizzie McGuire frowned as she played with the leopard-print pillow on her lap. She and her two best friends, Gordo and Miranda Sanchez, were having their usual three-way, before-school gabfest. Lizzie wished Gordo hadn't told her that he'd forgotten to tell her something. Now she'd spend the whole day wondering what that "something" was! And waiting for Gordo to remember things could take a long time.

"Oh, I know!" Miranda chimed in. "Was it about Lizzie's outfit? 'Cause it's, you know, not her fault red's not her color."

"Maybe because it clashed with the green spinach that was in my teeth all afternoon!" Lizzie cried, shuddering. Ugh, she thought, why did I ever think that I could have a spinach salad for lunch yesterday and get away with it?

"Is that what that was?" Gordo asked.

"I thought it was licorice," Miranda said.

Lizzie gaped at the receiver. Were her friends serious? Didn't they know that it was their duty to keep her from looking like a dweebaholic? "That doesn't matter!" Lizzie shouted. "The point is, you're my best friends. You should have told me."

Just then, the door to Lizzie's room swung open. Lizzie sat up straight on her bed, hugging the leopard-print pillow. Her annoying little brother, Matt, was standing in the doorway, cracking up. Lizzie's radar went off. Anything Matt found funny was, by definition, bad news.

"What, dog breath?" Lizzie said.

Matt just cracked up more. "Nothing."

Lizzie wanted to wipe the stupid grin off his face. She grabbed the pillow and tossed it at his head. Matt gasped and pulled the door closed just in time to avoid the assault.

"Freak!" Lizzie called after him.

"That's it!" Gordo said suddenly. "I just remembered what I'm supposed to tell you. Ethan said that if you wanted to sit with him at lunch today, he'd be cool with it."

"Ethan?" Lizzie asked, practically squealing. "Ethan Craft?" Ethan Craft was the most popular guy at Hillridge Junior High School, not to mention the absolute hottest. "He said I can eat lunch with him today? And you're telling me this *now*? *Way* into the conversation? With no time to prepare?" Lizzie looked down at her outfit—her favorite multicolored sweater and orange patterned pants. Not *too* bad. Maybe it wouldn't be her first choice as something to wear to have lunch with Ethan, but it would have to do. Thanks to Gordo's slow memory circuits, she didn't have time to pull together a totally new outfit.

"I couldn't remember," Gordo said defensively. "You want to know why? Because it's not that important!"

Lizzie snorted. "Not important?" she said.

"Gordo," Miranda said, "if Lizzie has lunch with Ethan, the whole school will notice."

"No, they won't," Gordo said.

Lizzie's mouth widened in shock. Not

because Gordo wasn't getting the magnitude of this whole Ethan Craft lunch thing—he never understood stuff like that—but because she had just realized that she had a problem on her hands—the phone was stuck to her ear. Only one person could be responsible for this: her weaselly brother, Matt. He had smeared honey all over the cordless phone, and now it was fastened to her head in a gooey mess.

"Yes, they will," Miranda went on, oblivious to Lizzie's struggle with the phone. "Which translates into being popular. Lizzie will be popular! Which means, *we* will be popular!"

"Whatever," Gordo said with a sigh.

Lizzie struggled to pull the phone away from her head. No luck. She decided to give it a good yank. Unfortunately, she pulled a little too hard, and wound up falling off the bed. *Thunk!*

"Lizzie?" Miranda said into the phone.

"What happened?" Gordo wanted to know.

Lizzie struggled to her knees. "Let's just say I have a problem. It's about four feet tall, it has brown hair, and it's far worse than your not telling me I had spinach stuck in my teeth all afternoon." She struggled with the phone a little more, but it remained fastened to her hair. "I'd hang up," she said, "but I can't."

Matt must have been switched at birth. My real brother couldn't be some prank-pulling, lizard-killing, make-believe-friend-having weirdo. i want a blood test!

Lizzie finally managed to pry the phone from the side of her head and click off. But her ear was still totally sticky. Gross! Now she was going to have to get this goo out of her hair—she didn't have time for a whole new shower—and she'd probably be late for school. Lizzie just hoped that the honey would come out. She couldn't possibly have lunch with Ethan looking like she'd walked face first into a beehive.

Grrr.

How did her little brother manage to be so incredibly annoying? It wasn't possible that they had the same genes.

Lizzie found her mom in the kitchen.

"Mom!" Lizzie yelled. "Look at what Matt did to my hair!" She pointed to the gooey side of her head.

"Oh, dear," Mrs. McGuire said. She motioned to a stool and had Lizzie sit down; then she hesitantly began to inspect the damage. "I don't think it's *too* bad," Lizzie's mom said. "Here, lean back."

She had Lizzie lean backward over the kitchen sink and used the sprayer to wash out the mess. Then she ran upstairs for a small towel and a mirror. "See?" Lizzie's mom said as she rubbed the wet patch of Lizzie's hair dry. She showed Lizzie her reflection in the mirror. "You're as good as new. No big deal."

"No big deal?" Lizzie demanded. "No big deal? But I'm supposed to have lunch with—" Lizzie stopped herself. There was only one thing that could possibly make this morning worse, and that was having to deal with her mom getting all misty-eyed over the fact that Lizzie was having lunch with a boy. "I am having a very important lunch today, Mom," Lizzie said, swallowing her impatience, "and now my hair is ruined!"

"Lizzie, I think we got almost all the honey out," Mrs. McGuire said. "I don't think anyone's going to notice."

"Yes they *will*," Lizzie countered, remembering the spinach incident from the day before—"they just won't say anything." Lizzie sighed. Really—couldn't she just have one day, *one day*, in which she went to school and didn't have to suffer utter humiliation?

Just then, Lizzie's dad walked into the kitchen.

"Well, let's ask your father," Mrs. McGuire said brightly. "Sam, look at Lizzie." Mrs. McGuire put her hands on her daughter's shoulders. "Doesn't she look *especially* nice today?" she prompted.

Mr. McGuire poured himself a cup of coffee. "Yeah, she does," he said, not even bothering to look at Lizzie—"especially her earrings." Lizzie's dad was never really awake until he had his first cup of coffee in the morning.

Poor Dad. He tries so hard but, most of the time, he's clueless.

Mrs. McGuire shook her head slightly.

"Uh, I mean, her outfit," Mr. McGuire corrected.

Mrs. McGuire winced and pointed to her daughter's head.

"Of course, your hair," Mr. McGuire said, finally getting it.

Lizzie rolled her eyes. "See?" she said to her mom. Obviously, her dad was totally lying.

"No, it looks nice," Lizzie's dad insisted. "Beautiful, in fact."

"See?" Mrs. McGuire said, as though her husband's opinion was utter proof that

Lizzie's hair was gorgeous. As though she hadn't just forced him into saying so!

Poor Mom. She's got Dad so well trained, she actually believed that.

"I'm telling you, Lanny, the honey thing worked great!" Matt said into the cordless phone as he wandered into the kitchen. "I did exactly what you said, but I used my sister instead of a hamster." He giggled a little, then turned around and gulped hard when he saw his entire family sitting there, staring at him. "Uh, Lanny, I gotta go," he said quickly, clicking off. "Hi!" he said, giving his family an innocent wave.

"If you wanna know what's good for you, you won't talk to me, you won't look at me, and you'll pretend you don't know me," Lizzie snapped at him.

"Forever?" Matt asked. He shrugged. "Works for me."

"Hey, Matt," Mr. McGuire said in a warning tone. "That's your sister. Be nice."

"But she's such an easy target, Dad," Matt said.

"Oh! Let's see if you can say that with your head underneath my foot!" Lizzie screeched, sliding off her stool and stomping toward Matt.

Mrs. McGuire hurried to step between her daughter and Matt. "Okay, that's it," she said, separating them. She pointed her finger at her son. "Matt, you are grounded."

"Yeah," Mr. McGuire agreed. In a low voice, he asked his wife, "What did he do?"

"Her hair," Mrs. McGuire whispered, jerking her head in Lizzie's direction.

"Oh, right." Mr. McGuire nodded.

Lizzie gritted her teeth. She *knew* her father had been lying!

"So what is it this time?" Matt asked in a bored voice. "No TV? No friends over after school?" He thought for a moment, then added hopefully, "No more chicken noodle casserole?"

"I know," Lizzie said suddenly. "Why don't we just send him away," she suggested. "Like, forever."

"That's not a bad idea," her mother agreed.

Lizzie's eyebrows flew up. She hadn't expected her mom to go for her idea so easily. Maybe I should suggest that she give me twenty bucks, Lizzie thought craftily.

"Hey, that's not very nice!" Matt whined.

"Well, you haven't been very nice, either, young man," Mrs. McGuire replied. "Putting honey on your sister's phone." She waved her hands at him, exasperated. "Just go to school. I'll deal with your punishment later."

"Ooh, I'll rush right home," Matt said sarcastically, his eyeballs rolling back into his head.

I wonder if he can see his tiny brain rolling around in there, Lizzie thought.

"Hey, Matt, cool it," Mr. McGuire said sternly. "All right? You better hurry up before you miss your bus."

Matt sighed, and looked at the floor, completely dejected.

He looked so sad that Lizzie actually felt kind of bad for him.

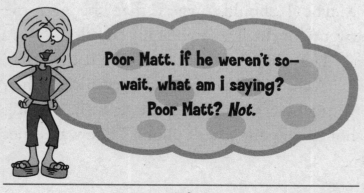

Poor Matt. if he weren't so—
wait, what am i saying?
Poor Matt? *Not.*

"Hey, what about her?" Matt demanded, pointing at Lizzie.

Lizzie planted her hands on her hips. "Mom's taking me to school, brother from another," she said haughtily.

"Ooh, 'Mommy's taking me to school,'" Matt mimicked in an annoying, little-kid voice.

Lizzie narrowed her eyes as Matt left the kitchen. Oh, well. What was the point of getting mad at him now? At least she was going to school, where she would have six whole Matt-free hours . . . not to mention lunch with Ethan!

This day was going to be great. It had "possibility" written all over it.

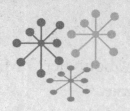

CHAPTER TWO

Matt plodded along toward the bus stop. He was definitely in no hurry to start his day, especially now that he had a punishment waiting for him at the end of it. But as Matt rounded the corner, his eye caught a flash of yellow. The school bus—it was already pulling away from the curb!

"Hey! Hey! Hey, wait for me!" Matt cried, running after the escaping bus. "Don't go!" Matt raced after the bus, his short legs pumping, his heavy backpack bouncing against his shoulder. "Wait!" He chased it for half a block before the driver finally noticed him and slowed down. "Thank you," Matt said as the bus hissed to a stop.

Matt climbed aboard and nodded absently at the bus driver. The bus pulled away as the doors slid shut behind him, and Matt made his way down the aisle, looking for his friends. But he didn't see Lanny or Oscar anywhere. In fact, none of the kids on the bus looked familiar. And most of them looked . . . older.

Suddenly, Matt's eyes grew wide as the truth hit him like a freight train. "Hey," he said out loud, "this isn't my bus!" Matt turned to escape out the front, but it was too late. The bus had already made a few turns. He couldn't possibly get off now. He was on his way to a strange school with a bunch of strange people, and there was nothing he could do about it!

Just as quickly as he had panicked, Matt calmed down and realized the situation wasn't so bad. "Oh, well," he said, sliding into a seat near the back.

Matt stared out the window, wondering vaguely where he was headed. The bus jerked to a stop, and a couple more kids stepped on.

A shadow fell over Matt, and he looked up into the face of Ethan Craft. Not that Matt knew who Ethan was. Or that he would have cared if he had known. But Ethan was pretty big, compared to Matt, and most other kids would have been frightened by the look Ethan was giving Matt at that moment.

"You're in my seat, little man." Ethan stared down at Matt threateningly. "Move it," he commanded.

Matt looked around. There were empty

seats everywhere. "Uh, I don't think so," Matt said.

"You don't think so?" Ethan repeated, glowering at Matt.

"Uh, no," Matt replied. He gave Ethan his most innocent look. "Unless I missed the sign that says RESERVED FOR FRANKENDORK."

Ethan gaped at him. "What?" he demanded.

"Franken. Dork," Matt said slowly, as though he were speaking to an idiot. "Frankendork. I'd show you, but I don't have a mirror."

Ethan glanced over his shoulder as some of the kids behind him started cracking up. "Who are you?" Ethan asked, turning back to Matt.

Matt cocked an eyebrow. "They call me Bond," he said in a cheesy, faux British accent. "Matt Bond."

Ethan frowned. He wasn't used to dealing with extra-small smart alecks on the bus. But he did have a few ideas as to how to handle this one. "All right," he said finally, cracking his knuckles, "you leave me no choice." He pounded his fist into his palm. "How do you want it?" he asked, leaning over Matt menacingly. Most kids shook in their shoes when Ethan threatened to get physical.

But Matt didn't look scared. He just glanced around, then shrugged. "Um, shaken, not stirred?" he suggested, reciting one of his favorite James Bond lines.

That actually cracked Ethan up. "You're funny," he said, laughing and shaking his head.

"So are you," Matt shot back. "But looks aren't everything." He smiled at Ethan.

Ethan grinned. "Slide over, Bond," he said. He wanted to find out what this kid's story was. He was sure that it was going to be pretty interesting.

Lizzie fiddled with her hair as she walked down the hall with Gordo and Miranda later that morning. She still wasn't sure that it looked okay, but she'd managed to do something with it, thanks to a few last minutes with some styling products and a curling iron. She just hoped that it looked good enough for lunchtime with Ethan Craft.

"Your hair looks fine," Gordo assured her for about the fiftieth time. "Really."

"Oh. And for the record, your teeth are clear, too," Miranda chimed in. Her dark hair was looking totally cute in high pigtails fastened with fuzzy pink ponytail holders, and Lizzie tried not to feel jealous that Miranda had a hairstyle that was completely honey-free.

"Thanks, Miranda," Lizzie said, rolling her

eyes. Why couldn't her best friend have given her the tooth update yesterday—when it mattered? Not that Lizzie was going to make a big deal out of it now. She had bigger fish to fry. "Anyway, I've made a decision. I'm not going to let my little brother ruin what is otherwise the greatest day of my entire life."

"What's so great about it?" Gordo asked as he followed Lizzie to her locker.

Lizzie shook her head. Gordo could be so dense sometimes. "Tell him, Miranda," Lizzie said as she yanked open her locker and reached for her English notebook.

"Two words, Gordo," Miranda said.

"If you say 'Ethan Craft,'" Gordo warned, "I swear I'm gonna hurl."

Miranda raised her eyebrows. "Fine," she shot back. "In that case, I'll say one word: lunch."

Gordo made a retching sound and put his

hands to his stomach, like he was going to barf. Lizzie shot him the look of death and slammed her locker shut. Honestly, Gordo could be so immature. But I'm not going to let it bother me, Lizzie told herself. Nothing can ruin this day. Nothing. Not a thing.

As long as my teeth stay clear.

"I hate writing on the chalkboard," Miranda complained to Lizzie as they walked toward their lockers after math class. "It makes my hands all powdery and dry. Like my grandma's face." She looked at Lizzie, who was staring straight ahead, with a dreamy smile on her face. Miranda waved her hand in front of Lizzie's face. "Hello?" Miranda said. "Anybody home?"

"Oh," Lizzie said as she snapped back to reality, "sorry." She gave Miranda an apologetic smile.

"Where is your head today?" Miranda wanted to know.

Lizzie giggled nervously. The truth was, she'd sort of been planning her wedding . . . to Ethan. True, they were only having lunch, but still—weddings take a lot of time to plan. It's best to start early! Not that she wanted to confess that to Miranda. "Oh, nowhere," Lizzie said with a smile.

"Hey, guys," Gordo said as he walked up to them.

"Hey, Gordo," Lizzie said.

"*Qué pasa?*" Miranda asked.

"Have you guys heard about this new kid?" Gordo asked, frowning.

"You mean the one with the recording contract?" Miranda asked. She looked annoyed. "Yes, I haven't *stopped* hearing about him." She turned to Lizzie and explained. "His parents are spies, he goes to Disney World at least twice a year, and he's already skipped three grades."

"Yeah, well how 'bout the fact that he's already made a movie! A *movie*!" Gordo ranted. "And not just any movie, but a feature film! With Steven Spielberg! And he's younger than I am! He's *younger*"—Gordo pointed to himself—"than me!"

"Whoa, whoa, whoa. Who is this kid, anyway?" Lizzie asked.

"I haven't met him yet," Miranda admitted, "but he's a friend of Ethan Craft's."

"Ethan?" Lizzie asked, giggling slightly. Any friend of Ethan's is . . . well . . . someone I may have to invite to my future wedding! Lizzie thought happily.

"He transferred here from some small, private school on an uncharted island near Fiji," Miranda went on as the three friends headed down the hallway. "His name is, uh, uh,"

Miranda said, scratching her head, thinking hard. "Matt something."

Lizzie froze in her tracks and grabbed Miranda's wrist. "Matt?" she repeated. "Please, don't say that name around me."

"I can't believe it," Gordo went on, clearly not listening to them. "Younger than me and he's already worked with Spielberg."

Just then, a classroom door flew open, whacking Lizzie in the face! Lizzie's papers went flying as she fell flat on her back. A crowd of kids poured out of the room, completely oblivious of Lizzie and her pain.

From her spot on the ground, Lizzie heard a familiar-sounding voice say, "So I said to him, *Harry Potter* should be seen, not just read, and that's why they're making the movie." Lizzie wondered whether the voice belonged to the new kid, as a bunch of other voices chorused their admiration. She was pretty sure that she heard Ethan's voice saying, "Way to go, Bond!"

"Lizzie!" Miranda said, kneeling over her friend.

"Are you okay?" Gordo asked.

Lizzie grabbed her head. "Yeah, I'm fine," she said woozily. "Was that . . ."—Lizzie glanced over her shoulder, but the crowd had already turned the corner—"was that Ethan? Did he say anything about lunch?" she asked hopefully.

Gordo and Miranda just looked at each other.

Okay, Lizzie thought, reading their expressions. I guess you could say that I'm definitely out to lunch!

CHAPTER THREE

"**O**h, Sam, this is all my fault!" Mrs. McGuire wailed as she hurried into the kitchen, where Mr. McGuire was busy at his computer.

"Hold on a second, honey," Mr. McGuire said. "I'm making a killing on this on-line auction, selling your old Leif Garrett records."

"Sam, I need you to listen to me," Mrs. McGuire said urgently. "It's Matt." Mrs. McGuire's voice was shaking. "He's missing.

His school just called. He never showed up. And the last thing I said to him before he went to school was that I thought that we should send him away forever." Her voice cracked with emotion. "And I think he thinks I hate him, and he ran away from home—I mean, from us, I mean . . ." She swallowed hard, and touched her chest. "From *me*!"

"Now, just slow down, all right, honey?" Mr. McGuire said soothingly. "This has happened before, remember? That time that Matt hid under the bed for an entire day so that he didn't have to do the square dancing during P.E.?"

Mrs. McGuire took a deep breath, remembering. Matt had worn a camouflage hat to blend in with the other junk under his bed.

"No, I checked under the bed!" Mrs. McGuire said. "And the only thing there was a week-old chicken noodle casserole." She bit her lip, holding back tears. "I thought he liked that, too."

"You know, he's gotta be around here somewhere," Mr. McGuire said confidently. "Do you remember the time he sneaked out so he could be the first in line at the toy store to meet Tarzan?"

"Yeah, he didn't sneak out," Mrs. McGuire said sheepishly.

"Huh?" her husband asked.

"I went with him," Mrs. McGuire admitted.

"I knew you liked that guy!" Mr. McGuire cried. "It was the way he was hanging from the rope, right? And the loincloth and all—"

"Okay, okay, okay!" Mrs. McGuire shouted. "This is serious! Matt's missing, and we have to find him!"

"Okay," Mr. McGuire said. "Look, you check the closets. I'll look under the house."

He pushed back his chair and headed out onto the patio.

Mrs. McGuire nodded, then hurried out of the kitchen. She was going to tear apart each and every closet in the house until she found her baby!

"Okay, this is it," Lizzie said excitedly, as she walked into the lunchroom with Miranda— "the moment I've been waiting for, for, like, my entire life. Lunch with Ethan Craft."

Just then, Lizzie spotted Ethan across the cafeteria. He was standing with a group of popular kids. He looked up, and gave Lizzie a nod and a smile.

"I want you to remember every detail," Miranda sputtered eagerly. She was so excited, she was practically sending saliva across the room. "Every expression, every word—"

"No worries, Miranda," Lizzie said, grabbing

Miranda's shoulders. "I'll tell you everything." She giggled.

"Spank you!" Miranda said, giggling, too.

Just then, Gordo walked up to them, carrying his lunch tray. "Okay, I wasn't going to say anything, but I think you need to hear this," he said to Lizzie. "The fact that you care so much about sitting with Ethan is kind of pathetic." Miranda and Lizzie exchanged glances as Gordo went on with his lecture. "So he's popular," Gordo admitted. "And maybe he's good-looking. So what? Who you are is way more important than who you sit with at lunch."

Lizzie looked him up and down skeptically. "You done?" she asked.

Gordo nodded.

"Good," Lizzie said. "Here I go!" She gave Miranda a hug.

"Good luck!" Miranda chirped.

"Hey, Lizzie, over here!" Ethan called out from his lunchroom table.

Lizzie gulped, picturing herself running toward Ethan on a silver cloud. This was a dream. No, it was better than a dream. It was . . .

The crowd Ethan was standing with let out a cheer. As Lizzie walked up to them, she saw that they were all gathered around an incredibly small kid, who was standing on a table, wiggling his butt. Someone had brought in a boom box, which was blaring dance music. Who is this guy, and what in the world is he doing? Lizzie wondered. Just then, the kid turned around and struck a pose on the table. "And that's how Britney learned to dance!" the kid announced.

Lizzie couldn't believe her eyes. The kid who was wiggling his butt on the table, the kid who was friends with Ethan Craft, was her annoying little brother. *Matt?* she thought. Matt! This was no dream—it was a *nightmare*!

That's when Matt noticed Lizzie. "Ahhh!" he screamed.

"Ahhh!" Lizzie screamed back.

The screaming went on and on.

Lizzie grabbed Matt by the front of his shirt and dragged him off the cafeteria table.

"What are you doing?" Matt demanded through clenched teeth as Lizzie led him away from the crowd.

"Getting my life back," Lizzie growled.

"Hey, don't worry," Matt called over his shoulder to the confused crowd of kids that stood watching him get hauled away. "I'll tell you how I was knighted by the queen when I get back." He winked and pointed a finger pistol at the crowd as Lizzie dragged him out the cafeteria door.

"What are you doing here?" Lizzie demanded once they were out in the hall.

Matt thought for a moment. "Well, see, it all started when—"

"Do Mom and Dad know that you're not in school?" Lizzie asked, cutting him off.

Matt gave Lizzie a condescending look. "But I *am* in—"

Suddenly, the truth crashed over Lizzie like a tidal wave, and she gasped. "*You're* the new kid, aren't you?"

Matt shrugged. "Well, it kind of looks that way, but—"

"Does anybody know that you're my brother?" Lizzie asked.

Kate Sanders, the most popular girl in

school, picked that moment to come sauntering by with her posse trailing behind her. Lizzie bit back a groan. Kate had been making Lizzie's life miserable ever since they hit junior high. She and Kate used to be friends, but once Kate became queen bee, she had no more use for unpopular drones like Lizzie.

"Well, at first I thought he did look kind of familiar," Kate said, loud enough for Lizzie to hear as she pranced past, "but then I thought, Lizzie could never be related to anybody that cool and charming." Kate caught sight of Matt and gave him a little wave. "Oh, hi, Matt," she said, batting her eyelashes. Then she turned and strutted into the cafeteria.

Lizzie cringed as her brother gave Kate a casual wave.

"Did Kate just call you 'cool'?" Lizzie asked Matt. Matt cocked an eyebrow and opened his mouth to reply, but Lizzie decided that she didn't want to hear the answer. "Never mind," she said quickly. "Here's the plan, we're gonna call Mom and Dad to pick you up, and by tomorrow, everyone will have forgotten who you are."

"Uh," Matt said slowly, "that's not going to work for me."

"What?" Lizzie gaped at him.

"I like it here," Matt explained. "The playground's bigger, the food's better, and everybody's really nice." Matt waved to some eighth grader who was walking by. "Especially that Ethan guy."

That Ethan guy? That Ethan guy?! is it too late to put Matt up for adoption?

Lizzie glared at Matt, completely speech-less. Was he really talking about her lunch date and potential husband that way?

"You know, all I ever hear you say about this place is how horrible it is," Matt went on. "But it's really not. I like it here." He put his hands on his hips. "I'm staying."

"No, you're not!" Lizzie cried, horrified at the very idea.

Matt opened his eyes wide. "Uh, yes, I am," he said in his best *duh* voice.

"No!" Lizzie screeched.

Luckily, Miranda and Gordo walked out of the cafeteria just in time to keep Lizzie from lunging at her little brother. As the door swung open, Lizzie could hear the kids chanting Matt's name, like he was some kind of rock star who owed them an encore.

Matt lifted his eyebrows knowingly. "The people," he said, "have spoken." Matt pushed his way past Miranda and Gordo, and swaggered through the cafeteria doors. A cheer went up as he entered the room.

Gordo stared after him a moment. "At the risk of sounding selfish, I, for one, am glad it's Matt," he said.

Lizzie's jaw dropped open. Had Gordo lost his mind?

"Steven Spielberg," Gordo said, chuckling to himself. "What an imagination."

"So, what are you going to do?" Miranda asked Lizzie.

Lizzie was too stressed to do anything but offer a feeble squeak in reply. But of course—there was only one solution to this problem.

What am i going to do? i'll do what any other red-blooded sibling would do. i'll go to Mom and Dad.

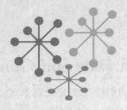

CHAPTER FOUR

Mr. and Mrs. McGuire stood in front of Matt's best friend, Lanny, who was seated on their couch. The McGuires had called the police and half of Matt's friends, but so far, they hadn't heard anything about where their son had gone. A police officer was in the kitchen, trying to get some information from headquarters. Meanwhile, the elementary school had let the McGuires pull Lanny out of class to see if he knew where Matt might be. But so far, the kid was being pretty tight-lipped. Not that that was unusual for Lanny. In fact, neither Mr. nor Mrs. McGuire could ever remember having heard him utter so much as a peep. Then again, Matt spent hours on the phone with Lanny—so they knew he must talk sometimes. Or at least, they *hoped* he talked sometimes.

"So," Mr. McGuire said, "did Matt say anything about not going to school today, Lanny?"

Lanny shook his head.

Mrs. McGuire looked at him accusingly. "You were on the phone with him this morning," she pointed out.

Lanny shrugged.

Mr. and Mrs. McGuire looked at each other, then leaned toward Lanny. "Nothing about square dancing or missing a test?" Mr. McGuire suggested.

Lanny thought for a moment, then nodded.

"Yeah?" Mr. McGuire asked eagerly.

Lanny looked around, reconsidering, then shook his head no.

Mr. and Mrs. McGuire straightened up. "The kid's not talking," Mr. McGuire whispered.

"Does he ever?" Mrs. McGuire demanded through clenched teeth.

"He's one of Matt's best friends," Mr. McGuire said. They both turned to look at Lanny, who had folded his arms across the couch's armrest, and was staring intently at the gnome lamp that stood on the side table.

"That's not saying much," Mrs. McGuire said with a sigh.

Just then, the police officer walked into the living room.

"I just checked with headquarters," he

announced, hooking his thumbs through his belt. "They're gonna circulate some pictures, canvas the area. Don't worry, in cases like this, it's best to just sit tight. We'll know something soon." He glanced over at Lanny, who was still staring at the gnome. Lanny looked up at the officer and cocked an eyebrow. "You're right," the officer said. "Gnomes are weird." Then he shook his head and walked back into the kitchen.

Mr. and Mrs. McGuire stared at each other. Maybe they should have had the police officer question Lanny!

"But they never let us make phone calls from the principal's office," Miranda protested as she walked down the stairs next to Lizzie.

"Are we or are we not allowed to use the school phone in case of emergencies?" Lizzie demanded, not even breaking her stride.

"Allowed," Miranda admitted reluctantly.

"And, being my best friend and knowing how I feel about him, do you or do you not think that Matt's being here is an emergency?" Lizzie asked.

"Well, see," Miranda said uncomfortably, "that's where you and I differ."

Lizzie swung around to look her friend in the eye. "Miranda," she griped, stomping her foot, "it's *Matt*. The best thing about going to school every day is the fact that he's *not* going to be there!"

"But for the first time in our lives, we can use him to our advantage," Miranda insisted.

Lizzie folded her arms across her chest and looked at her friend skeptically. "No, thanks."

"But Matt's a friend of Ethan's," Miranda said, "which makes Matt popular. *We* want to be popular. Matt could help us."

"Help us?" Lizzie couldn't believe her ears.

"He's already ruined my lunch with Ethan Craft. Besides, I don't even care anymore. I just want him gone!"

Miranda nodded, as though she understood, then shook her head. "This all made sense to me before we started talking."

"Well, while you're trying to make sense of it, I'll be in the office, using the school phone," Lizzie snapped. "Later." She turned on her heel and strode away dramatically —colliding face first with an open locker door. She fell to the ground.

"You see?" Matt said as he climbed out of the locker. "As long as you can hold your breath, being stuffed inside a locker isn't really that bad." He turned to two geeks and motioned for one of them to step inside. "Here, you try it." As one geek stepped into the locker, Matt noticed Lizzie glaring up at him from the floor.

"Hel-lo," Matt singsonged cheerfully, giving her a little wave.

Lizzie hauled herself to her feet. Matt didn't hesitate; he turned and ran as Lizzie chased after him. As she ran past the locker, her elbow caught the door, slamming it shut.

Miranda started after Lizzie.

"Um, hello?" said a muffled voice from inside the locker. "Anybody?"

Miranda looked at the locker, then shrugged and kept walking.

Not her brother. Not her locker. Not her problem.

Lizzie walked into the main office and glanced around. Good—the coast was clear. She reached over the front desk and pulled out the phone. She had just picked up the receiver and begun to punch in her home phone number when Principal Tweedy walked out of his private office . . . with Matt. Thinking that her brother had been busted, Lizzie started to smile—then she noticed that there was something definitely wrong with this picture. Principal Tweedy was grinning. And he had his arm around Matt. Not good. Lizzie hid the phone behind her back.

"The way that you've explained it," Principal Tweedy said to Matt, "I see no reason why scooters shouldn't be a part of the P.E. curriculum. I'm gonna bring it up with the board."

Lizzie gulped when Principal Tweedy noticed her. "Now, you know the rules, Ms. McGuire," he said. "No student phone calls."

"But this is an emergency," Lizzie insisted, gesturing toward Matt. "I mean, my little brother's at my school!"

"Yes, he is," Principal Tweedy said as he

patted Matt on the back, "and we're very lucky to have him."

Matt gave Lizzie a triumphant look.

"But he doesn't belong here!" Lizzie cried.

"You're right," Principal Tweedy said. He looked at Matt and smiled. "He belongs in the gifted program."

"You don't understand," Lizzie said, shaking her head.

"Oh, but I do. And just a tip, Lizzie," the principal said, patronizingly—"jealousy isn't pretty on a girl. Let's try and work through it."

Matt started to crack up.

Lizzie decided that it was time to take the direct approach. "Excuse me," she said, holding out the phone to Principal Tweedy. "Can you just call my parents? I'm sure they're really worried about him." Let's see what the principal has to say about my "jealousy" when he gets an earful from Mom, Lizzie thought happily.

"Uh, no," Matt said quickly, patting the principal on the shoulders, "you don't have to do that."

"Actually, I was gonna do that right now," Principal Tweedy said. He held up a Rolodex card and took the phone from Lizzie, who shot Matt a victorious smirk.

"You are so busted," Lizzie whispered as Matt began to bang his head against the desk.

Principal Tweedy finished dialing and waited. "It's the machine," he said after a moment.

Matt lifted his head from the desk. "Yes!" he hissed.

"Hello," the principal said into the phone, "this is Principal Tweedy from Lizzie's school. Just wanted to call and say what a joy it is having Matt here with us today." Matt flashed Lizzie an evil grin.

Somebody, wake me up! Please, anybody, wake me up from this horrible nightmare!

Lizzie gave herself a pinch, but it didn't help. This was really happening. And there was no way out!

Okay, Lizzie thought, the only way to fix this situation is to go to extreme measures. She scanned the hall as she hurried toward social studies class. Bingo. Ethan was just heading into the classroom. And there's still three minutes until the bell, Lizzie thought. Plenty of time to rat Matt out.

"Hi, Ethan," Lizzie said as she slipped into the chair next to his.

"Hey, Lizzie," Ethan said, looking up at her with a smile.

How should I begin? Lizzie wondered, taking a deep breath. She decided to just dive right in. "So, I just thought I should tell you," Lizzie began, jiggling her leg tensely, "Matt's not who you think he is. I just thought you should know that." She let out a nervous giggle, which she hoped didn't sound too dorky.

Ethan's eyebrows drew together. "Weird," he said slowly. "The little guy *said* you'd do something like this."

Lizzie frowned. "He *did*?"

Ethan stared at her.

Please, don't let him be staring at the honey patch on my head, Lizzie begged silently. "Something wrong?" Lizzie asked, giggling nervously again.

"Nah, I was just wondering, does your brain hurt, like, all the time?" Ethan asked.

"My *brain*?" Lizzie asked, rolling her eyes. This conversation was getting majorly weird.

"I never met anybody with permanent brain freeze," Ethan went on. "Mine just lasts, like, a minute."

"What are you talking about?" Lizzie asked. I don't have brain freeze! she thought. Where could Ethan have gotten an idea like . . . ? Wait a minute. "What else did that little Matt say about me?"

"About your eyes," Ethan said, leaning in closer.

Lizzie felt her cheeks get hot. Was it possible that her brother had actually said something nice about her—like, that she had beautiful eyes? Ethan was staring at her so intently, what else could it mean? "What about my eyes?" Lizzie asked hopefully. If Matt said something really nice, Lizzie thought, I might just let him live.

"Does the one really pop all the way out of your head when you get mad?" Ethan asked.

That's it! Matt's going down!

Lizzie was completely speechless. Ethan actually thought that she had brain dysfunction and freakish eyes? Okay, no more Ms. Nice Girl, she decided. It was definitely time to pull out the heavy artillery.

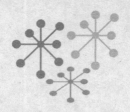

CHAPTER FIVE

Mr. and Mrs. McGuire paced back and forth in the kitchen while the police officer sat at the table, sipping coffee and munching a doughnut. He'd had three already.

"Well, this is ridiculous!" Mrs. McGuire said finally. "I can't stand here, waiting. I'm going nuts!"

"Isn't there something we can do?" Mr. McGuire asked the officer.

"It's best to just stay home and wait for the

phone to ring," the police officer assured him. "Other than that," he added brightly, holding out his mug, "I'd love some more coffee."

"No," Mrs. McGuire shouted. She slapped her hand down on the kitchen table. "No! I'm not making you any more coffee until you can tell me where my baby is!"

All of a sudden, Mr. McGuire remembered what he had done. "Wait a second!" he said. "I turned the phone off when I was on-line and—"

Mrs. McGuire stared at him. "What?" she demanded. "It's been off this whole time?" She ran over to the answering machine.

"Well, I was wheeling and dealing," Mr. McGuire explained defensively, hurrying after her. "You know, 'cause Leif Garrett records are really hot these days." He looked down at the machine, which was blinking. "Oh, look, messages!"

Mrs. McGuire glared at him, then sighed and pressed PLAY. The first message was from Mrs. McGuire's mother. Mrs. McGuire rolled her eyes and fast-forwarded to the next message. "I'll deal with her later," she said.

There was a beep, then Principal Tweedy's voice spilled from the machine. "Hello, this is Principal Tweedy from Lizzie's school—" Mrs. McGuire pressed FAST FORWARD. "Lizzie's school?" she moaned. "I don't have time for you—my baby's missing!" But that was the end of the messages. "That's the last message?" Mrs. McGuire said, sniffling a little. "But I wanted to hear from Matt. I want my Matty!" she wailed, hugging the machine against her chest. "I want my Matty!"

Mr. McGuire wrapped her into a big hug. "Honey, it's going to be okay," he reassured her. "It's gonna be fine."

"Um," the police officer interrupted, pointing toward the kitchen, "that coffee?"

"And voilà," Matt said as he sat on a lab table in Lizzie's science class—"the perfect meal." Matt lifted the lid off a metal crucible and showed off what he had concocted to the small crowd of kids that had gathered around him. They burst into applause. "I'll be sharing more recipes on *Oprah* next month," he told them.

Lizzie sighed and tapped her pen impatiently against her notebook.

"There you are," Miranda said as she and Gordo strode into the room.

"You okay?" Gordo asked, leaning against Lizzie's lab table.

"Never better, actually," Lizzie said with a smile.

"Why the sudden turnaround?" Miranda asked suspiciously.

Gordo leaned against the lab table and frowned. "Yeah, I heard Principal Tweedy busted you."

Lizzie looked at the ceiling and smiled innocently. "It was worth it."

"Say what?' Miranda asked.

"While Principal Tweedy was showing Matt around the school, I sneaked in and used his phone to call—" But Lizzie never finished her sentence, because just then, two uniformed police officers walked into the classroom. She turned around to look at Matt, who was in the middle of yet another one of his stories.

"So I said, "'Tissue? I hardly know you. . . .'" Matt grinned as the crowd of kids cracked up.

The tall police officer looked at Matt dubiously. "Matt McGuire?" he asked.

When Matt saw the policeman, his eyes

went wide. "No," he said quickly in a phony British accent. "No Matt McGuire here."

The officer looked down at the pad of paper in his hand and tried again. "Bond?" he asked. "Matt Bond?"

Matt pressed his lips together. "I guess the jig is up," he said dramatically as he slithered down from the lab table. He placed his hands behind his head. "Go easy on me, would you, fellas?"

Lizzie giggled as the police escorted her brother from the classroom. Talk about getting stone-cold busted!

Woo-hoo! Yeah!

"Wow!" said a kid at the front of the classroom. "Matt's getting arrested!"

"How cool!" someone else said. The crowd murmured their admiration as Matt and the police walked out the door.

What? I just can't win today! Now I've made him even *more* popular.

Lizzie groaned and put her head on her lab table.

"Well, you know what they say," Miranda said, her chin in her palm. "Tomorrow is another day."

"That may be true," Gordo piped in, "but Matt's *always* going to be her brother."

Miranda giggled as Lizzie glared at Gordo. "Thanks," Lizzie said. "Way to spread the sunshine, Gordo."

Gordo grinned. Then he shook his head and chuckled. "Spielberg," he said. He slapped the lab table and walked out of the room.

"It's okay," Miranda said, putting a sympathetic arm around her friend. "I feel for you."

Lizzie sighed. Nobody could possibly understand the pain of having Matt for a brother. Nobody. He'd actually managed to destroy a day full of possibilities!

And I thought a little tooth spinach was bad, Lizzie thought. At least she had managed to floss that away. Matt was going to stick around . . . forever!

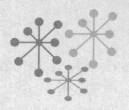

CHAPTER SIX

"So, did Matt get in beaucoup trouble?" Gordo asked later that night when he, Miranda, and Lizzie were on a three-way call.

Lizzie grinned in satisfaction. "Total. Grounded for a month—no TV, no phone, and the best part is, he's got to keep a solid ten feet away from me at all times."

"Yeah, but meanwhile, everyone at school is still talking about him," Miranda said with a sigh.

"Yup, nothing says 'cool' like getting arrested," Gordo chimed in sarcastically. "Especially at school."

Lizzie's phone beeped. "Oh, hold on," she said, "I got another call, guys." She clicked over. "Hello?"

"Lizzie?" someone said. Lizzie's heart started pounding like crazy. She knew that voice!

"Hi, it's Ethan."

"Ethan," Lizzie said, trying to sound as casual as possible. "Hi. Um—can you hold on a second?" She clicked back over to her friends. "Omigosh, you guys," she said breathlessly. "Ethan! It's Ethan Craft. He's on the other line!"

"Ethan?" Miranda squealed.

"Omigosh, I gotta go!" Lizzie said quickly. How many seconds have gone by since I clicked over? Lizzie wondered, hoping desperately that Ethan hadn't hung up.

"Ethan!" Miranda repeated. "Oooh, Lizzie, I so want to be you!"

"Can someone please explain this guy's appeal to me?" Gordo asked, sounding bored.

Lizzie bit back a groan and clicked off. Let Miranda explain it to Gordo. Lizzie had important people to talk to!

"I'm back," Lizzie said to Ethan as soon as she clicked over. Omigosh, she thought giddily. Maybe he wants to ask me to sit next to him at lunch tomorrow, since Matt ruined our plans today! "So, what's up?"

"Hey, listen," Ethan said. "I was wondering. . . . What are you doing for lunch on Saturday?"

Lizzie grinned. Lunch on *Saturday*? Even better. That was practically a *date*! Her heart fluttered. Ethan is asking me out! she thought. "Uh, nothing," she said. "Yet."

"So then you'll have time to . . ."

Lizzie's heart skipped a beat.

". . . pick up a pizza for me and Matt," Ethan finished happily. "I *love* that little guy."

What? Ethan wanted to hang out with . . . Matt? "That'd be, that'd be great," Lizzie snapped, "but I think that's when Matt's nap time is. Later." She clicked off and sighed, throwing her head back. Unfortunately, she threw it a little too far back and fell off the bed. "Ow!" she cried.

Matt ruined the best phone call of my life! it's not over. i'll get him.

"Watch out, little brother," Lizzie said from the floor. "I'll get you . . ." With a sigh she stared up at the ceiling and added—". . . one of these days."

Lizzie McGUiRE

PART TWO

CHAPTER ONE

"**F**ace it, Miranda," Lizzie McGuire said into the phone. It was after dinner and she had been in her room chatting with Miranda and Gordo for the past twenty minutes. "It doesn't matter which X-Man you are. You could be Mystique, that hot blue chick, and Ethan Craft wouldn't give you the time of day. Which is why *I'd* be Rogue. I'd use my mutant power to suck away all of Kate's popularity." Lizzie smiled smugly at the receiver, imagining the scene: her mortal enemy, Kate

Sanders, suddenly reduced from queen bee to wanna-be. Lizzie would stand there triumphantly while Ethan Craft panted at her feet. "Ethan would have no choice but to turn to me."

"Or *moi*," Miranda pointed out.

"Great," Gordo said sarcastically. "Use the untapped powers of the universe to land a guy who's gonna end up working at a gas station. *Part-time*."

Lizzie let out an insulted gasp. Gordo was a good friend, but he was a guy, and he had no appreciation for Ethan's utter hottitude.

Just then, the door swung open behind Lizzie. "Hel-lo? Ever heard of knocking?" Lizzie demanded as her annoying little brother, Matt, strode into her room. He was covered in dirt and carrying a shovel, which was pretty weird—even for him.

"Have you seen the flashlight?" Matt asked

as he yanked open Lizzie's dresser drawers.

"No," Lizzie said, staring at him. She crossed the room and slammed the drawers shut. Lizzie pointed to the phone, which she was still holding to her ear. "On the phone," she singsonged to Matt. "Leave."

Matt pulled open another dresser drawer, and Lizzie finally realized that her X-Man conversation was going to have to wait while she dealt with the dark forces of the universe that had just invaded her bedroom.

"Ugh!" Lizzie groaned into the receiver. "I have to get off the phone and crush my little brother." She clicked off and followed Matt to the other end of her room, where he was investigating the pile of dirty clothes on top of Lizzie's wicker hamper.

He dug through the clothes, tossing them aside recklessly. Lizzie shrieked as a green shirt landed on her shoulder. A moment later, a pair of blue patterned pants flopped onto her head. "You have five seconds till I sit on your head," she told her little brother through gritted teeth. "One . . . two . . ."

Matt continued to dump clothes on the floor, completely ignoring her.

"Three . . ." Lizzie continued.

"Got it!" Matt said cheerfully as he pulled the small black flashlight from the bottom of the hamper, where it had been hidden beneath the pile of laundry. He waved the flashlight in Lizzie's face triumphantly and jogged out the door just as Lizzie's dad wandered in.

"Does anyone knock in this house?" Lizzie demanded as she yanked the pair of pants off her head.

Mr. McGuire flashed his daughter a guilty look, then walked back to the door and rapped on it softly.

"Yes, Dad," Lizzie said with a forced smile as she brushed wisps of hair away from her face. Thanks to the pants that had landed on her head, Lizzie's blond hair now looked like a bird's nest topped with a hot-pink headband. "What do you want?"

"Do you have any idea why your little brother is covered in dirt?" Mr. McGuire asked.

Lizzie folded her arms across her chest. Honestly, why would her dad think that she had any idea why Matt did *anything*? "You caught me," she said sarcastically. "I buried him in the backyard, and he dug his way out."

Mr. McGuire's eyes went wide in shock.

"Joke!" Lizzie cried.

Her dad raised his eyebrows, but Lizzie couldn't tell if he thought the joke wasn't funny, or if he thought she might actually have tried to bury Matt in the backyard.

Come to think of it, Lizzie thought, I wish that I'd had that idea earlier. It has potential.

"I don't know why he's Mud Boy," Lizzie went on, "but I've got a lot to worry about, Dad. I'm getting married in the morning, so would you please excuse me?" Lizzie stormed off as her dad's mouth dropped open.

Mr. McGuire stood in the middle of Lizzie's room, clearly stunned by his daughter's wedding plans. "Honey?" he called weakly to his wife. "I need a little help!"

"The rules for the social-studies marriage project are as follows," Mrs. Stebel said later that morning as she passed out stacks of green handouts to the first person in every row. "I will pair you off into couples, and then everyone will come and select an occupation from this fishbowl." She held up a large round fishbowl that was full of brightly colored slips of paper.

Lizzie and Miranda smiled at each other, then glanced over at Ethan. Lizzie sighed, hoping desperately that Ethan would be her partner for the marriage project. He was just so gorgeous, and he looked even hotter than usual today. His sandy brown hair seemed to glow beneath the fluorescent school lights.

"Each couple must create a fictional lifestyle for themselves," Mrs. Stebel went on as she held up the fishbowl at the front of the room. Lizzie really liked Mrs. Stebel, their social studies teacher. She wore funky clothes and big, dangly earrings, and her hair was styled in supercool shortie dreds. She was always trying to think up creative projects for the class. And, in Lizzie's humble opinion, this project was definitely cool, since it came with the possibility of marrying Ethan! "And the couple with the best marriage *doesn't* have to write a paper," Mrs. Stebel added.

Lizzie lifted her eyebrows and wrote that down in her notebook. She definitely wanted to work hard on her marriage so she wouldn't have to write the paper! On the other hand, writing a paper could, potentially, equal more time with Ethan. . . .

"Each couple must make all decisions together," Mrs. Stebel went on. "The project will last one week and end with a pretend twentieth school-reunion party where you'll give a report about your last twenty years." Mrs. Stebel looked around the room. "Any questions?"

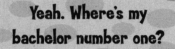

Yeah. Where's my bachelor number one?

The whole class was quiet.

"Okay," Mrs. Stebel said as she settled

behind her desk, "let's begin." She looked down at her notepad. "Kate Sanders."

Ugh, Lizzie thought as she watched Kate sit up eagerly and glance over at Ethan with a confident smile. Kate had gotten dressed up for today's assignment. She was wearing a sparkly white sweater with fluffy feathers at the wrists over a white T-shirt with a silver glitter heart on the front. She even had a sparkly barrette in her hair. Lizzie looked down at her powder blue vinyl jacket. Sure, it was cool, but it didn't really say, "World's Most Perfect Bride," the way Kate's outfit did. Lizzie sighed.

"Kate, you will be married to—" Mrs. Stebel looked down at her notes. Suddenly, Lizzie's heart started to pound. What if *Kate* ended up married to Ethan? Oh, no. That couldn't happen. It just couldn't!

"Larry Tudgeman," Mrs. Stebel finished.

Lizzie had to stifle a giggle as she watched Larry pull his finger out of his nose and give Kate a friendly wave. Larry was a sweet guy, but he was a total superdweeb. He always wore the same putty-colored shirt with the lime green collar, and he rarely found time to wash his hair. Lizzie could practically read the horror on Kate's face as she looked over in Larry's direction. Lizzie and Miranda grinned at each other. This was perfect!

Mr. and Mrs. Larry Tudgeman. Mrs. Kate Tudgeman. Kate Sanders-Tudgeman. It's all good.

"Mrs. Stebel," Kate said as she raised her hand in the air, "I can't be married to Larry." She flashed Larry a look of utter disgust as he happily went back to picking his nose.

Mrs. Stebel looked at Kate from beneath tired lids. "But you *are* married to Larry," she said.

Lizzie and Miranda looked at each other and giggled. Even Gordo was smiling.

"Stop saying that!" Kate insisted. "I want a new husband."

"There are no new husbands, Kate," Mrs. Stebel said patiently. "Now you and Larry come on up here and select your jobs." She pointed to the fishbowl at the edge of her desk.

This is great. i could be married to a tree frog and still have a better marriage than Kate.

Larry and Kate walked up to Mrs. Stebel's desk. They both reached into the fishbowl at the same time. When Kate's hand touched Larry's, she drew it back, then wiped it on Larry's shirt, as if trying to get rid of his cooties. She flipped her long, blond hair over her shoulders disdainfully.

Larry ignored her and pulled a pink slip of paper from the bowl. "Yeah!" he said eagerly as he glanced at the slip of paper. "Hey, I'm a mailman! No, no," he said, deepening his voice, "I'm a mail *delivery*man. For without me, there is no mail. I am the Mail Man." He punched his fist in the air.

Kate sighed and pulled a slip from the bowl. "I'm a TV anchorwoman," she read. Kate's expression changed completely. She smiled, putting her hand to her throat and gazing off into space, as though picturing her brilliant future. "I *love* that!" she said breathlessly.

"Honey, that's so great," Larry said, giving Kate a pat on the shoulder.

Kate slapped Larry's hand away. "Put a cork in it, Tudgeman," she snapped. Then she gave him a haughty look, turned on her heel, and strode back to her seat.

"All right," Mrs. Stebel went on, "Lizzie McGuire?"

Lizzie sat up eagerly and gazed at the back of Ethan's head in an attempt to make him her husband, using the energy of her mind. If only she had that X-Man power!

"Lizzie, you'll be paired with . . ." Mrs. Stebel looked down at her yellow pad.

Ethan Craft, Ethan Craft, Ethan Craft, Ethan Craft, Ethan Craft . . .

". . . David Gordon," Mrs. Stebel read. The name was so unexpected that, for a moment, Lizzie wasn't even sure she'd heard it right. Gordo? Lizzie peeked over at her best friend, who looked about as surprised as she felt.

Gordo's cool. Yeah, i'm seein' it. Best friends equals best marriage. Mix those two together and we have a recipe for victory. No paper for us this weekend. Yes!

Gordo waggled his eyebrows at Lizzie, and she giggled as they hauled themselves out from behind their desks and made their way to the career fishbowl.

Lizzie picked first. "Lawyer," she said as she read from her paper. She grinned. "Cool Moe Dee."

Gordo plucked his paper from the bowl. "Sanitation engineer."

Lizzie winced as Gordo groaned, but she couldn't help giggling a little.

"Oh, no, I'm a garbageman," Gordo said. "I'm Gordo the garbageman." He shook his head and turned back toward his desk. "My wife's a lawyer," he said. "I pick up trash."

"Hey." Larry reached out and grabbed Gordo's arm. "It doesn't make you less of a man. Trust me, I know." He pointed to where Kate sat, inspecting her perfect French manicure. "My wife?" Larry whispered. "TV personality."

Gordo rolled his eyes and walked back to his desk.

"Miranda Sanchez," Mrs. Stebel announced, "you'll be paired with Ethan Craft."

Lizzie's mouth dropped open in shock. So did Kate's. And so did Miranda's.

Okay, she's my best friend, so i guess i'm happy for her. But this is so unfair.

Miranda turned to Lizzie, clearly stunned, then walked unsteadily to the front of the class to pull her occupation from the bowl.

Ethan smiled at Miranda as she reached Mrs. Stebel's desk. "Hey, Mrs. Ethan Craft," he said to her casually as he reached toward the fishbowl.

Miranda had to press her lips together to keep from grinning like crazy. She looked over at Lizzie, who gave her a thumbs-up as Ethan pulled a slip of paper from the bowl.

"Surgeon," Ethan read. He looked blankly at Mrs. Stebel. "That's, like, a doctor, right?"

Okay, so i've met vegetables brighter than Ethan. But he is a total hottie.

"He's a doctor," Gordo grumbled in disbelief, "and I'm a garbageman." He dropped his pen on his desk and shook his head.

Miranda looked down at her piece of paper. "Homemaker," she read. She gave a satisfied little shrug, then folded the paper and slipped it into her pocket.

Ethan held out his elbow to Miranda. "Can I escort Mrs. Ethan Craft to her seat?" he asked, flashing her a megawatt smile.

Kate glared at them, pouting, as Ethan walked Miranda back to her desk. Lizzie tried to smile. After all, she didn't want to be like

Kate. She wanted to feel happy for her best friend. Really. But everything about this project was just so unfair!

Miranda laced her arm through Ethan's and grinned. "That's Mrs. *Doctor* Ethan Craft," she corrected him.

Mrs. Doctor Ethan Craft?

Ugh. Things were getting worse by the minute.

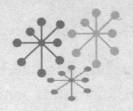

CHAPTER TWO

"Hey!" Miranda called as she walked over to where Lizzie and Gordo were sitting together at their usual table in the atrium. Lizzie looked up and smiled at her friend, but Miranda didn't sit down. "I just wanted to let you guys know I'm eating with my *husband the doctor* today," Miranda said, holding out her hand. Lizzie had to squint. Miranda was wearing the biggest cubic zirconia Lizzie had ever seen. That is, she *hoped* it was a cubic zirconia. It was as big as her eyeball! "See you guys in the gym?" Miranda said as she waggled her fingers in front of Lizzie, then made a face, smiled, and walked away.

"Did you see the rock on Miranda's hand?" Lizzie asked Gordo as Miranda hurried over to where Ethan sat on the other side of the atrium.

Gordo just rolled his eyes.

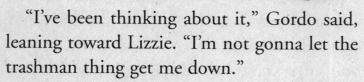

That's not a rock— it's a continent.

"I've been thinking about it," Gordo said, leaning toward Lizzie. "I'm not gonna let the trashman thing get me down."

Lizzie sighed, and peered over at the table where Miranda was sitting next to Ethan. Lizzie felt a pang of jealousy as Ethan laughed at something Miranda said. What could

Miranda have said that was so funny? Lizzie wondered. Ethan should be sitting with me, she thought, laughing at *my* jokes!

Lizzie wished that Gordo would be quiet, so that she could hear what Ethan and Miranda were talking about. But Gordo was on a roll, droning on and on about his career as a sanitation engineer. "And I've got plans," Gordo added. "Big plans. I'm gonna build a trash empire. With employees and trucks and city contracts. It's gonna be huge."

Just then, Lizzie heard a voice behind her. "Hey, Kate?"

Lizzie turned and saw Larry standing next to the queen bee herself. He was holding a cafeteria tray loaded down with today's special: meat loaf and brussels sprouts. I can't believe he got the sprouts, Lizzie thought as she watched Larry stand there, waiting for Kate to notice him.

Kate didn't. She completely ignored Larry, pretending to inspect her perfect French manicure.

"Kate?" Larry said, more loudly this time.

Kate sighed, but didn't even look up at Larry. "Do I know you?" she asked.

"Uh, yeah," Larry replied patiently. "I'm your husband?"

Kate went back to inspecting her nails.

"Mrs. Stebel's class?" Larry went on. "The mailman?" He plopped his tray onto the table and slid into the empty seat next to Kate. "Okay," he said. "We should probably get to work on this."

"Look," Kate said nastily, "I have plans this weekend, so I can't write a paper, so I need the best marriage, which means *you* can't be in it." She put her dainty hand in Larry's face. "Okay?" Kate waved to someone across the cafeteria.

Larry speared something on his plate and held it out to Kate. "Brussels sprout?" he offered.

"Ew!" Kate cried. She moved away from him and flailed at the gross-smelling sprout.

Lizzie laughed. Who knew that brussels sprouts could be put to such good use?

"The key is one truck," Gordo droned on, cutting into Lizzie's people-watching. "Just one garbage truck. And that becomes two garbage trucks."

Lizzie glanced over at Miranda and Ethan again. They were giggling at something. Oh, aren't we just so hilarious today? Lizzie thought jealously.

"Then three," Gordo went on. "Then a lot of garbage trucks. A fleet of garbage trucks. For, you see, trucks equal contracts, and contracts equal money, and money equals power."

Lizzie watched as Ethan offered Miranda a

French fry, and she took it with a shy smile. *Grr.* Is that fair? Lizzie thought. Miranda gets Ethan and French fries, and I have to sit here, listening to Gordo's lecture on the possibilities of garbage?

"Are you even listening to me?" Gordo asked suddenly. He snapped his fingers in front of Lizzie's face. "Hello!" he called.

"Uh. Yeah," Lizzie said vaguely, tearing her eyes away from Dr. and Mrs. Ethan Craft. "You're talking about trash." She glanced over at her best friend, who was smiling as Ethan picked at his lunch.

"You know, Lizzie, I know we're friends, but sometimes I feel like you take me for granted," Gordo said. He leaned in to get her to notice him. "Like *now.*"

Lizzie snapped back to attention. "What?" she asked.

"How do you think that makes me feel?"

Gordo asked. "We've been married for less than a period, and you're already jealous of someone else's husband."

"I'm not jealous!" Lizzie insisted.

"We have to work on this marriage thing together," Gordo told her.

> i'm not jealous. She's Mrs. Doctor Ethan Craft. i'm married to a trashman. i am not jealous.

Lizzie nodded. Gordo was right. She knew he was . . . but she couldn't help sneaking just one more look at Miranda and Ethan.

Lizzie was propped on a stool at the kitchen table, doing her homework, when Matt ran into the kitchen. He yanked open the fridge, grabbed some root beer and beef jerky, and stuffed them into a small red cooler. Then he slammed the fridge closed and ran out onto the patio. Lizzie didn't even look up. More weirdness from her brother—and she did not want to get involved.

"Honey?" Mrs. McGuire called after Matt as she walked into the kitchen. He ignored her, so she turned to Lizzie. "Lizzie?" her mom said in a low voice as she leaned against the table where Lizzie was working. "Do you know where your brother's going?"

"Mom," Lizzie said, lifting her eyebrows. "I'm his sister. We don't talk."

"I'm just worried," Lizzie's mom said absently as she watched Matt out on the patio. "He's been really good lately. But, like, *too* good. Are you sure you haven't noticed anything weird?"

"Hmm." Lizzie pretended to think for a moment. "Besides his troll-like appearance and his distaste for hygiene, no. Anyway, I've got enough to worry about. Miranda gets to be Mrs. Doctor Ethan Craft, and I get to be married to Gordo, the trash king."

Mrs. McGuire gaped at her daughter.

"Oh, school project," Lizzie explained. "Don't worry."

Lizzie's mom planted her hands on her hips. "Listen," she said, "I don't know what your teacher is telling you, but marriage is not about how much you earn or what you have. It's about love." She put her hand across her heart. "And trust. And communication. Right, honey?" she asked as Lizzie's dad walked into the kitchen and grabbed an apple from the fruit bowl.

"Huh?" Mr. McGuire said as he polished the apple on his shirt.

"Just say yes," Mrs. McGuire told him.

"Yes," Mr. McGuire said obediently.

Mrs. McGuire gave her husband a peck on the cheek. "Good boy."

Okay. Nice that my parents like each other. But gross when they kiss in front of me.

"I'm so outta here," Lizzie said as she flipped her notebook shut. She grimaced as she walked out of the kitchen, leaving her lovebird parents to smooch it up in her absence.

"Honey, I'm worried about Matt," Mrs. McGuire said as she watched Matt gather his things and leave the patio. "I think you should go follow him."

"I'll get my coat," Mr. McGuire said, putting his apple back on the counter. He grabbed his jacket from a peg in the hall, hurried outside, and followed his son across the backyard and through a wide field until he came to some woods. Mr. McGuire had to dodge branches and leaves as he followed his son's path through the thick trees. After a few minutes, Matt seemed to disappear. Mr. McGuire was about to give up and turn back when he noticed a large hole in the side of a hill. A shower of dirt came flying out of it.

Mr. McGuire peered into the hole, just as a pile of dirt landed in his face. Mr. McGuire spat the soil out of his mouth and crawled deeper into the cave, just as another pile of dirt smacked him in the face. He shook his head and crawled into the hole, which, it turned out, was a cave large enough to stand up in. Matt was in one corner, wearing a baseball cap with a flashlight duct-taped to the front, shoveling dirt.

"Matt?" Mr. McGuire called as he crawled into the cave. "Hey, Matt. Hi." He gave Matt a little wave. "What are you doing here?"

Matt looked surprised to see his father. "Uh. Tidying up my cave," he explained uncomfortably.

Mr. McGuire looked around, still on his knees, as he brushed the dirt from his clothes. "Is that what this is?"

"Uh. Yeah," Matt said.

"I didn't know there was a cave up here," Mr. McGuire said. He adjusted his glasses, which had been knocked askew by the dirt.

"There wasn't," Matt told him.

Mr. McGuire's eyebrows flew up as he gazed at his son. "You mean, you made this cave?"

"I dug it," Matt said.

Mr. McGuire looked around, clearly impressed. The cave was pretty big. "Wow," he said. "Well, how long did it take you?"

"I dunno." Matt shrugged. "Couple of weeks?"

Mr. McGuire looked around again, this time, in confusion. "Why?" he asked.

"Well, you see, I ran into these rocks," Matt said, pointing behind him.

"No, Matt." Mr. McGuire shook his head. "What I mean is, why did you dig a cave?"

"Dad, haven't you ever wanted a place that's your own?" Matt asked. "A place you can just hang?"

Mr. McGuire thought about that for a moment. "Each and every day of my life, son," he admitted.

"Are you gonna tell Mom?" Matt asked.

"Well," Mr. McGuire said, "you have parental supervision, so that would make this okay."

Matt and his dad looked at each other for a moment. Then Matt smiled and handed his dad a shovel. "Welcome to the Matt Cave," he said.

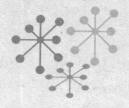

CHAPTER THREE

Lizzie headed over to her favorite cybercafé, the Digital Bean, to study. While I'm here, I might as well get one of their delicious Superberry smoothies, Lizzie thought as she went up to the counter and placed her order with the lanky, dark-haired waitress. There was no point in studying on an empty stomach. While she waited for the drink, Lizzie scouted around for a place to sit. Suddenly, her eye fell on a couple in the corner who looked very cozy. The girl flipped her hair, and Lizzie felt her stomach drop. She knew those two!

Kate. Ethan.
Probably totally innocent. Wait. It's Kate. Definitely not totally innocent.

Kate leaned flirtatiously toward Ethan and took a sip from the smoothie they were sharing. Lizzie frowned. This did not look good. She had to find out what was going on!

Lizzie spotted a garbage can behind Kate and Ethan. Thinking fast, she grabbed a tray filled with empty plates and used cups and napkins and oh-so-casually made her way over toward the garbage can, which was conveniently hidden behind a column between her and Kate. Garbage is really the theme of my life lately, Lizzie thought, as she peered around the column to get a look at the cozy couple.

"So what I was thinking . . ." Kate started to say, as she leaned toward Ethan. Lizzie bent toward them to hear more, and accidentally tipped over the tray she was holding. One of the drinks spilled, and when Lizzie tried to step away from the mess, she slipped and fell flat on her back!

Unbelievably, Kate was so wrapped up in Ethan that she didn't even notice. "I was thinking that Mrs. Stebel clearly made a mistake with my marriage. So I'm planning to leave Larry at the reunion."

Lizzie hauled herself off the floor and crawled around the column until she was under Kate and Ethan's table. Ugh. Now she had a gorgeous view of Kate's perfect pedicure, and of the gum stuck to the underside of the table.

Ethan thought about this for a moment. "Does that mean I get . . . two wives?" he asked eagerly.

"No," Kate said slowly. "But if you leave Miranda, then you and I could be married."

What? Lizzie couldn't believe what she was hearing. Kate was going to double-cross her own husband—and Miranda! But would Ethan go along with it? Even though she knew that Ethan and Kate could discover her at any minute, Lizzie couldn't leave yet.

Still, the floor was a very uncomfortable place to sit. She adjusted her position so that she was leaning against the table leg, and hit her head against the underside of the table. Ouch! Now her head hurt, and her hair was caught in a gross wad of used chewing gum! Mega-ick! And even worse—how was she going to ever get out from under this table without ripping half of the hair out of her head?

"Oh," Ethan said finally. "That's still cool."

Lizzie tried to pull her hair out of the gum, but it wouldn't budge. It was like it was stuck there with industrial cement or something!

"How's that sound, Dr. Craft?" Kate asked craftily.

Ethan laughed. "You're really smart," he said.

Just then, the lanky waitress stepped out from behind the counter and peered around the café. Please, don't let her see me, Lizzie begged silently. Please!

Spotting Lizzie under the counter, the waitress walked over and delivered Lizzie's smoothie. "Excuse me," the waitress said, leaning under the table, "here's your drink."

Lizzie grimaced, then took the drink. After all, what choice did she have? Thanks to the gum, she was permanently stuck to this table. Just stay cool, Lizzie told herself. Maybe nobody will notice. "Thanks."

Kate and Ethan peered under the table. Lizzie winced, then smiled at them feebly. "Hi," she said, and took a sip of her drink, as though she liked to hang out underneath café tables all the time.

i would give a year's allowance to be anyplace but here right now. Maybe two years'.

"Garbage is gold," Gordo said as he scribbled something onto a piece of paper. "Stinky gold, but gold nonetheless."

"Whatever." Lizzie flopped backward onto the couch in her family's living room. Gordo had been talking nonstop about garbage for the past ten minutes. He had come over to her house to work on their marriage project, which was quickly turning into the David

Gordon Trashtacular. He had brought a ton of notes and articles, all about the sanitation industry. In Lizzie's opinion, Gordo had a serious case of trash on the brain.

"C'mon, Lizzie," Gordo begged, "give me a hand here." He gestured toward his garbage notes. "I mean—you want the perfect marriage, and you've been making zero effort."

"Gordo, quit nagging me!" Lizzie griped.

"*Nagging* you?" Gordo repeated, as though he couldn't believe what Lizzie had just said. "I wouldn't have to nag you if you paid attention to me."

"I'd pay attention to you if you talked about something other than garbage," Lizzie snapped back.

"Like what?" Gordo asked patiently.

"Ethan and Miranda," Lizzie said.

Gordo nodded, as though he understood perfectly. "Mmm."

Lizzie rolled her eyes. What was that "*mmm*" noise supposed to mean? She knew that Gordo just thought that Lizzie was bummed because she would rather be Mrs. Dr. Ethan Craft than Mrs. Garbage-Obsession. But that wasn't the problem at all! Well, it wasn't the *entire* problem.

"You know trash might not be glamorous, Lizzie," Gordo said, "but it's gonna put our kids through school."

"That's not it," Lizzie said impatiently.

"Then what is it?" Gordo asked.

"I went to the Digital Bean yesterday and I saw Ethan—with *Kate*," Lizzie explained. "Kate's planning to leave Larry at the reunion. And she wants Ethan to do the same to Miranda."

Gordo frowned. "But it's just a school project," he said. "It's not real."

"It'll be real to Miranda when she gets

dumped in front of the entire class," Lizzie pointed out.

"Okay. You're right," Gordo admitted. "We have to tell her before the reunion."

Lizzie looked at the ceiling. "How do we do that?"

"You have to talk to her," Gordo said gently.

Lizzie sighed. Gordo was right, and she knew it. There was only one problem. How in the world was Lizzie going to tell Miranda?

"There's a bunch of batteries in the garage," Mr. McGuire said as he and Matt hurried into the kitchen, "and I think there's more beef jerky in the pantry."

"Hey!" Mrs. McGuire called, jogging after them.

Mr. McGuire and Matt stopped in their tracks as Mrs. McGuire gaped at the mud and dirt caked all over their clothes.

"Sam," Mrs. McGuire said slowly, "can I talk to you for a second?"

"Sure," Mr. McGuire replied. He leaned toward Matt and whispered something in his ear.

"Got it," Matt said and scurried out of the kitchen.

Mr. McGuire turned back to his wife and grinned at her innocently.

"What's going on?" Mrs. McGuire asked. Her eyebrows drew together.

"Nothing," Mr. McGuire said quickly. "Just a little male-bonding time. With me and Matt." He cleared his throat uncomfortably, then turned and strode out of the room.

Mrs. McGuire stared after him for a moment, clearly confused. "You know I'm gonna find out!" she called after him. But her husband was already long gone.

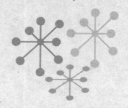

CHAPTER FOUR

Lizzie glanced around the Digital Bean. When she'd called Miranda's house earlier, her mom had said that Miranda was at the cyber-café. Lizzie and Gordo had hurried over there so that Lizzie could break the lousy 4–1–1 about Kate and Ethan's plan. But half of Lizzie was hoping that her friend wouldn't be there. She hated giving people bad news.

Suddenly, Lizzie spotted a familiar-looking head of dark hair. Miranda was sitting at a table by herself. It's now or never, Lizzie thought as she hurried over. She wanted to get this heinous conversation over with as quickly as possible. "Hey, Miranda!" Lizzie said as she slid into the empty chair across from her friend. "Haven't seen you around."

"Yeah, being a doctor's wife can be pretty hectic," Miranda said with a smile. She took a sip from her drink and put it back on the table.

Lizzie giggled nervously. "So," she said uncomfortably, "how's that working for you?" She couldn't help noticing that Miranda was doing something new with her hair. She looked really good. She probably did it to impress Ethan, Lizzie thought, stifling a flash of anger. How could Ethan treat her friend this way? It wasn't fair—not when Miranda was so sweet and nice and fun.

"We've decided that Ethan's a heart surgeon,"

Miranda said, grinning. "We have three kids: Britney, Gwyneth, and Ethan Junior. I drive the kids to soccer practice in my metallic-blue SUV with beige leather interior." Miranda lifted her eyebrows and sat back in her chair, smiling at her fantasy.

"And what about Ethan?" Lizzie asked.

Miranda shrugged. "Oh, he works a lot. Heart surgeons do, you know. But he'll meet me here later." She picked up her soda and took a small sip. "This project is so much fun."

"Great," Lizzie lied. She pressed her lips together, wishing that she could just duck out of there. Miranda looked so happy. Lizzie didn't want to be the one to ruin her best friend's perfect fantasy life, complete with an SUV and kids with trendy names. But if she didn't tell Miranda what was really going on, Lizzie would just have to watch Miranda's life come crashing down around her in Mrs. Stebel's class. I have to tell her the truth, Lizzie decided. Right now. "Miranda," Lizzie said miserably, "I have to tell you something—"

"Hey, ladies!" a voice cried, interrupting Lizzie. "Dr. E's in the house!" Lizzie looked up just in time to see Ethan striding toward them. He settled onto the stool beside Miranda, who giggled happily.

i am so erasing his name from my notebook.

"Sorry I'm late," Ethan said to Miranda. "I had some doctor stuff to do," he joked, putting finger-quotation marks around the word "doctor." Lizzie had to bite her lip to keep from telling him that she'd hoped he'd been giving himself a personality transplant.

Miranda nodded at Ethan, then turned back to Lizzie. "You were saying, Lizzie?" she asked.

Miranda smiled at her, expectantly. Lizzie glanced uncomfortably at Ethan, then turned back to Miranda. Just tell her, Lizzie thought. Tell her now! "Um. I was saying . . . that I'm meeting Gordo here, so, I have to go." Lizzie shoved back her chair and walked away quickly.

I'm not a coward. Really. it's just not the right time.

Oh, help! Lizzie thought as she joined Gordo by the snack counter.

"I hope you guys are as happy as we are!" Miranda called, waving at Lizzie and Gordo.

Gordo shot Lizzie a dubious look. "She, uh, doesn't look too upset," he said hopefully.

Lizzie groaned in frustration. "That's because she doesn't know," she snapped. She glanced over at her friend, who was grinning widely at Ethan. "I couldn't tell her," Lizzie admitted. "I mean, she looks so *happy*."

"You know, the longer you wait, the more hurt she's going to get," Gordo pointed out.

I'm such a wimp.

"You're right," Lizzie said. She shook her head. "I just don't know how I'm going to break it to her."

Gordo patted Lizzie on the shoulder. "You'll think of something," he said.

Lizzie sighed. She sure hoped that he was right.

Meanwhile, back at the cave, Mr. McGuire and Matt were munching on string cheese and reclining on beach chairs. Mr. McGuire was wearing an old football helmet with a flashlight duct-taped to the front, while Matt had on his baseball cap/flashlight headgear. They had spent the afternoon making a few cave drawings with sidewalk chalk—until the art project turned into a duel with chalk sabers. Then they had guzzled root beer until Matt complained he had a stomachache. After that, they lit a bunch of little candles around the cave and sat down to relax in their cheery glow.

"Dad, does it get much better than this?" Matt asked with a contented sigh. He tossed a rubber ball in the air, then caught it again.

"Nope," Mr. McGuire said between bites of string cheese. "It doesn't." He looked around the cave. "You know, I've been thinking. What we really need is some more room."

Matt lifted his eyebrows. "Talk to me."

Mr. McGuire pointed to a spot just behind Matt. "I could blow that wall out another seven feet. Then we'd have enough room in here for a generator. We could have indoor lights."

"And TV," Matt added. "Can't forget TV."

"Yeah, TV'd be cool," Mr. McGuire agreed. He looked around, then up at the ceiling. "We could probably punch a hole in the roof here . . . bring in some satellite."

"Cool!" Matt smiled at his dad.

"How big a screen do you think we could get in here?" Mr. McGuire mused.

"Sam? Matt!" Mr. McGuire looked over, and saw Mrs. McGuire's head poking into the entrance to their secret lair! "What are you guys doing in there?" she demanded. "Get out of this mud hole, right now."

"But—" Matt and Mr. McGuire chorused.

"No, no buts," Mrs. McGuire said, cutting them off. She shook her head. "This thing could collapse on you any minute! Come on."

"But it's cool!" Matt complained.

"I know it's cool, honey," Mrs. McGuire replied, "but it's dangerous." She looked at her husband. "Right, Sam?"

Mr. McGuire sighed.

"Right, Sam?" Mrs. McGuire prompted again.

Mr. McGuire thought for a moment, then

turned to Matt. "Son," he said, "she caught us fair and square. At this point, resistance is futile." He turned off the flashlight strapped to his helmet, as a signal of defeat.

"Women," Matt said sadly. "You can't live with 'em—you can't let 'em know where your cave is."

CHAPTER FIVE

"I cannot believe you're wearing that," Lizzie said to Gordo. She frowned at the dirty pair of garbage-green overalls he had on. Gordo's fashion taste usually ran to the extreme, but an authentic garbageman outfit was a bit much, even for Gordo.

Gordo and Lizzie were standing together in the gym, which Mrs. Stebel had decorated with balloons and a big banner that read MRS. STEBEL'S 20TH CLASS REUNION. Mrs. Stebel had gone all out for the occasion. She had even laid out little sandwiches and a big bowl of punch on a long table at the rear of the gym. All of the students were dressed up in costumes to represent their careers. Lizzie was wearing a dark blue suit, and had her hair pulled back neatly in what she thought of as a "lawyerly" do. But did Gordo really have to go totally all out?

"I'm a trashman," Gordo protested as he looked down at his coveralls. "I'm proud of where I come from."

Lizzie shook her head. She had hoped that her husband would have dressed up for the occasion—maybe even worn a suit. After all, wasn't he supposed to be the *head* of a garbage empire? Did he really have to dress like he'd just finished having lunch with Oscar the Grouch? "Don't you care if we win?" Lizzie asked.

"No, I don't," Gordo admitted. "Not any-more."

Lizzie looked at him, hugging her notebook against her chest. What is Gordo talking about? she wondered. He'd been working hard on this project all week. He *had* to care!

"I care that ever since we got married, you just seem annoyed by me," Gordo went on. "I care that I feel like my best friend is taking me for granted."

Lizzie sighed. Gordo was right—as usual. She really hadn't been a very good friend to him. What is up with me lately? Lizzie wondered, thinking about how she'd failed Miranda the day before.

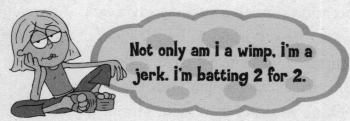

A movement caught Lizzie's eye, and she turned to see Miranda walk into the gym with

Ethan. Miranda was wearing a housedress and apron, and even had a kerchief over her dark hair. Ethan was in mint-green scrubs. Miranda folded her arms across her chest as she listened to Frankie Wallis and Sally Falconer finish up their report. Frankie was dressed as a farmer, while Sally had on police blues.

"So, basically, while I was out milking cows, she was in the big city, fightin' crime. . . ." Frankie explained.

"But I was home on weekends," Sally went on, "and we had three kids."

Lizzie wasn't paying attention to the report. Her eyes were locked on Ethan and Miranda. She saw Ethan waggle his eyebrows at someone, and turned just in time to see Kate give him a conspiratorial wave. Lizzie narrowed her eyes.

"Commuter marriage," Mrs. Stebel said, nodding appreciatively at Frankie and Sally.

"Interesting." She looked down at her clipboard. "So, next up we have Kate Sanders and Larry Tudgeman," she announced.

Kate turned and daintily made her way to the stage. Lizzie frowned at her. Kate was wearing a pink suit and carrying a fake microphone. She had even teased her hair until she looked like a beauty pageant contestant after electroshock therapy. It was some serious helmet hair. Larry had on a regulation U.S. Postal Service outfit, complete with pith helmet and messenger bag stuffed with mail. Lizzie had to hand it to Larry—his outfit looked completely authentic. She couldn't help wondering if he had made it himself. Or maybe he'd just bribed a mailman.

Onstage, Larry leaned in toward the microphone, but Kate snatched it away from him. "I left Larry the day after our wedding," she announced snidely. "Of course, there were no children. I replaced Katie Couric on the *Today* show and won several Emmys. I lived fabulously ever after," she said, gesturing grandly. Larry gaped at her as she went on, "The end. Do I win?" Kate turned to Mrs. Stebel and smiled eagerly.

"Uh, I do not remember agreeing to any of that," Larry said into the microphone.

Kate sighed, throwing her head back dramatically, as though a husband as nerdy as hers couldn't possibly be asked to remember anything.

Lizzie winced. This was way embarrassing—and she wasn't even Larry's friend! Lizzie sneaked a glance at Miranda, who looked like she couldn't believe what a witch Kate was being.

"Kate, Larry, I want to see you after the presentations, please," Mrs. Stebel said stiffly. She frowned at Kate for a moment, clearly not amused, then looked back at her clipboard. "After a five-minute break, next up will be Miranda Sanchez and Ethan Craft."

Miranda put down her glass of punch and grabbed Ethan's arm eagerly. He quickly finished chewing the mini-sandwich he had just stuffed into his mouth and followed Miranda as she led the way toward the stage.

Lizzie took a deep breath. She couldn't let this happen. She couldn't let Miranda get dumped the way Larry had been! Not when she could stop it. Lizzie started after her friend.

"Wait." Gordo held out his hand in a stop gesture. "Where are you going?"

"To tell her," Lizzie explained. "I have to. I can't let her be humiliated in front of the entire class. I mean, sure, she's been Mrs. Doctor Ethan Craft for a week. But Miranda's been my friend for much longer. I can't just let her walk into this." Gordo nodded, and Lizzie hurried after Miranda.

"Hey, Miranda," Lizzie said quickly, as she stepped in front of Miranda, "can I talk to you for a sec?'

"Can't it wait?" Miranda asked, glancing toward the stage. "I'm about to give my report."

"No," Lizzie said firmly, "it can't."

Miranda turned to Ethan. "Give us a sec."

"Sure thing, sweetheart," Ethan said, giving her a sly wink. Miranda blew Ethan a little kiss. Ugh, Lizzie thought, as she watched Ethan amble toward the stage. This whole situation is enough to make me lose my lunch.

"Okay, Miranda," Lizzie said in a low voice, "Ethan is going to leave you. Like, now."

Miranda crossed her arms and narrowed her eyes. "Just because you're jealous doesn't give you the right to make stuff up," she said angrily.

"Miranda, I'm not making it up," Lizzie said earnestly. "I'm your friend."

"Yeah?" Miranda said angrily. "Some friend you are."

"Some friend *I* am?" Lizzie demanded, gesturing toward smarmy Ethan and his stupid doctor outfit. "One lame school project and you're spending all your time waiting around for some guy who doesn't even care about you, and who's going to leave you and embarrass you in front of the entire class!"

"What are you talking about?" Miranda asked, giving her hair a little flip. "Ethan and I spend tons of time together."

"No," Lizzie replied. "Ethan spends a ton of time with *Kate*."

Miranda's mouth fell open, and she seemed to deflate a bit.

Lizzie bit her lip, but she knew that she had to force herself to go on. Miranda needed to know the whole story. "I saw them at the Digital Bean together," Lizzie explained. "Kate asked Ethan to leave you at the reunion, just like she left Larry." Miranda looked as though she had just been punched in the stomach. Lizzie hated hurting her friend, but what else could she do? "I tried to tell you," Lizzie said apologetically, "but you seemed so happy."

"What?" Miranda asked. Her voice was thick with emotion. "How?"

Lizzie shook her head. "I'm really sorry."

"Yo! Is there a Mrs. Doctor in the house?" Ethan said into the microphone.

Slowly, Miranda turned to face the stage. She looked a little sick. She hesitated a moment, then squared her shoulders and walked toward her "husband."

Lizzie's heart was aching. She wished that she could do something for her friend. But she had just done the only thing she could. The rest was up to Miranda.

Ethan leaned toward the mike as Miranda took the stage. "Me and Miranda had our, uh, issues," he said into the microphone. "Y'know, like on *Ricki Lake*."

"Ethan was a heart surgeon," Miranda added mechanically. "I was a housewife. We had three kids. Britney, Gwyneth, and Ethan Junior. We had a vacation house. A swimming pool." She looked down at the floor. "I thought we had a pretty good life," she added quietly.

Ethan reached for the microphone, but Miranda snatched it away from him. "But Ethan was seeing someone else," she said angrily. "Weren't you, Ethan?" She narrowed her eyes at him accusingly.

"Uh, no," Ethan hedged. He turned pale, and Lizzie was pretty sure he was remembering all of the afternoons he had spent with Kate.

Miranda ignored him. "Ethan was going to leave me for Kate," she explained to the class. "But, you see, *Doctor*, that's not how I operate. I'm leaving you." Miranda poked Ethan in the chest. "You can take the car, you can take everything, but you can't take my *dignity*. I can't be married to someone who can't even manage to be my friend." Miranda threw the microphone on the floor and ran out of the room.

Ethan stood there, dumbfounded.

Lizzie felt like clapping. Miranda had totally made Ethan look like the jerk he had been!

There was a small shriek of feedback as Ethan picked up the microphone. "Uh . . . *Kate*?" he asked, frowning in confusion. "I thought I was gonna have *two* wives. . . . Now I've got none."

Lizzie rolled her eyes, and looked around to see Kate's reaction. But Kate wasn't even paying attention to Ethan. She was too busy griping at Larry over by the punch bowl.

"Kate, we need to go talk to Mrs. Stebel," Larry said.

"You better keep your mouth shut and agree that all of our decisions were mutual," Kate said, pointing a finger in Larry's face. "I'm *not* writing a report because you're a lousy husband." She jabbed him in the shoulder, knocking his hat askew.

"Oh, I'm a lousy husband?" Larry said, snatching his hat from his head. "Well, maybe if you'd just worked with me on this like I asked and the rules said, we wouldn't have this problem."

"Fine." Kate sneered. "I'll work with you. This marriage is over. How's that work for you?" She turned her back on Larry and folded her arms across her chest. "Now pour me some punch," she commanded.

Larry stared at the floor a minute, clearly stunned. "Yeah," he said finally, sighing in resignation. "Yeah, I'll pour you some punch." He placed his helmet on the refreshment table and took the ladle out of the punch bowl. Then he hauled the bowl off the table . . . and dumped the punch all over Kate! Sticky red punch splashed all over Kate's giant hairdo, deflating it, and dribbled all over her pink suit. The class cracked up as Kate stood there, soggy and humiliated, wiping gummy strands of hair off her face. It was the first time that Lizzie had ever seen Kate completely speechless!

"*Now* this marriage is over," Larry announced. He patted Kate on the back, then walked out of the gym.

Gordo turned to Lizzie. "I guess that's the

risk you take when you marry a postal worker," he said.

Lizzie winced, but she had to laugh. Witnessing Kate get her comeuppance from the Tudge was priceless. This was sure to cheer up Miranda!

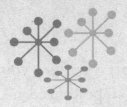

CHAPTER SIX

"I can't believe Ethan was gonna leave me," Miranda said over the phone later that night. She sounded pretty bummed. "It had to happen, right?"

"Yeah," Lizzie and Gordo agreed gently. Lizzie and her best buds were having their usual three-way, school-night chat. Even though Lizzie felt bad for Miranda, she was glad that things were back to normal with her friends.

"Well, I'm sorry I blew you guys off for Ethan," Miranda apologized.

"Well, now you know who your real friends are," Gordo pointed out.

"That was some speech you gave, Miranda," Lizzie added, hoping that it would make her friend feel better.

"Yeah, well," Miranda said, "I have my real friends to thank for that."

"I can't believe you didn't win," Lizzie went on.

"I *know*," Miranda agreed. "And I never thought the cop and the farmer would take it."

"A commuter marriage," Gordo scoffed. "How difficult was that? I mean, Lizzie, you and I, we had some real issues that we worked through."

"And we still have five hundred words due on Monday," Lizzie complained. Ugh. It was so unfair!

"So, what are you guys gonna write?" Miranda wanted to know.

"I think I might write about not taking people for granted," Lizzie said, "and being really lucky when you can marry your best friend."

"Oh, great, you realize this *now*?" Gordo demanded. "Where was that a couple of hours ago? We could've won with that!"

"Yeah, well, I'm waiting a really, really long time before I get married," Miranda said.

"Yeah," Lizzie agreed. "I think we're too young to even *pretend* we're married."

"I agree," Gordo said seriously. "But my trash empire could have been something big."

Lizzie gaped at the phone. There was silence at the other end. Miranda was clearly speechless, too.

"Hello?" Gordon's voice barked from the receiver. "Hello?"

Lizzie clicked off, giggling. She knew that Miranda would do the same. "Guys," Lizzie said, shaking her head.

Gordo stared at his receiver, wondering why his best friends had just hung up. "Chicks," he said with a sigh.

Lizzie grinned at the receiver. Even if she and Gordo hadn't won the marriage project, she was glad that she had friends as cool as Miranda and Gordo.

That was the most important thing, anyway. By a long shot.

Adapted by Jasmine Jones

Based on the television series, "Lizzie McGuire", created by Terri Minsky

Part One is based on a teleplay written by Douglas Tuber & Tim Maile

Part Two is based on a teleplay written by Melissa Gould

New York

Lizzie McGuire

PART ONE

CHAPTER ONE

"**M**ail's here," Mrs. McGuire said as she strode out onto the patio.

Lizzie McGuire looked up eagerly at her mom. But Mrs. McGuire sorted through the stack of envelopes without even glancing in Lizzie's direction.

Sighing, Lizzie leaned against her lounge chair and went back to leafing through the fashion magazine in her lap. Why do I even bother getting my hopes up? Lizzie wondered.

I never get any mail. Sometimes I wonder whether people even know that I live here. It's like I don't exist!

"Here you go," Mrs. McGuire said as she passed Lizzie's dad a small bundle of mail. He and Lizzie's annoying little brother, Matt, had been fixing Matt's old bike. Both of them were covered in grease. Mr. McGuire left black fingerprints on the envelopes as he flipped through them.

"Oh, good. Property tax bill," Mr. McGuire said sarcastically. He flipped to the next envelope in the pile.

Lizzie smiled a little behind her magazine. Okay, so there were some things that were worse than getting *no* mail.

"Matt got something from Gammy McGuire." Mrs. McGuire passed Matt a thick yellow envelope; then she looked down at what was left in her hands. "That's all junk,"

she said, flipping through it. "Junk, junk, junk."

Matt ripped open his card. "Cool!" he squealed. "A fifty-dollar gift certificate for my birthday!"

"But your birthday was seven months ago," Mr. McGuire said, clearly confused. He turned to his wife. "Gammy got him a baseball glove, right?" he asked.

Mrs. McGuire peered at him over the top of her square glasses. "Your mother sends him birthday presents every six weeks now," she said, then turned back to her enormous stack of junk mail. "She's getting a little . . . fuzzy around the edges."

Lizzie listened to this conversation distractedly as she peered at her magazine. Personally, she *liked* getting a birthday present from her grandmother every six weeks. It made a girl feel special.

Suddenly, Lizzie's eye fell on a full-page ad of a bunch of girls in cute dresses. They were running down the beach together. "Do you have Teen Attitude?" the ad read. "Then try out for our latest fashion show!" The address for the tryout was a store at the local mall. And it wasn't just any store—the fashion show was going to be held at Cielo Drive, home of the most bangin' outfits in town. Lizzie could hardly ever afford to buy anything there, but she liked to visit the shop on Saturdays and drool over the clothes.

"Hey, Mom, can I be a model?" Lizzie asked.

"Sure," Matt said, "and I can be president of the moon."

"Fine," Lizzie quipped, "as long as you move there."

Leaning forward, Lizzie showed her mom the ad and said, "*Teen Attitude* magazine is

putting on a fashion show at Cielo Drive. If I get picked, I get five hundred dollars' worth of free merchandise."

How cool would it be to get five hundred dollars' worth of stylin' clothes? Lizzie thought. She imagined herself waltzing into school, wearing a to-die-for outfit, grinning as her snob-alicious ex-friend Kate Sanders gritted her teeth with envy. Ha!

"If I say yes, will you stop picking on your brother and do all of your homework?" Mrs. McGuire asked. She looked at her daughter expectantly.

Pfft! Like *that's* gonna happen!

"Sure," Lizzie said, smiling innocently. She

sighed and leaned back in her lounge chair. "This is so cool," she said happily. "I'm going to be a model!"

Matt lifted his eyebrows at her. "I got fifty bucks," he said.

Lizzie rolled her eyes. Okay, so she wished she'd gotten fifty bucks in the mail, too. But modeling would be way cooler.

If it worked out.

"So they just had me walk down the catwalk and spin around twice," Lizzie explained to her two best friends, Miranda Sanchez and David "Gordo" Gordon, as they headed down the hallway at school the next day.

"Let me get this straight," Gordo said, frowning slightly. "You're going to be in a fashion show?"

"Yup," Lizzie told him. "And I get five hundred dollars' worth of free merchandise."

Miranda lifted her dark eyebrows, clearly impressed.

"Five hundred simoleons," Gordo repeated. "Why didn't you tell me about this thing?" he asked Lizzie accusingly.

Lizzie gave Gordo's outfit the once-over. It consisted of a wrinkled "vintage" print button-down worn over an ancient, red long-sleeved shirt, which hung, untucked and sloppy-looking, over a pair of painter's pants. Gordo was not exactly a fashionista, to put it mildly. In fact, school rumors suggested the fashion police had a warrant out for his arrest.

"I didn't think you'd be very interested in a fashion show," Lizzie said, giving Gordo a dubious look.

"I wouldn't be," Gordo agreed. "But for five hundred skins, I'd volunteer for scientific experiments."

Lizzie grinned, picturing Gordo and a

Labrador hooked up to some crazy brain-switching device. Then she tried to imagine Gordo strutting down the runway in a tux. Somehow, it *did* seem more likely that Gordo could make money as a guinea pig for science than as a male model.

"I thought to be a model, you had to scowl and stomp around like you own the place," Miranda said.

"I just walked," Lizzie said with a shrug. "They said I seemed like a nice, typical teen girl."

"You *are* a nice, typical teen girl," Gordo told her.

Lizzie glared at him. *Typical?* Ouch!

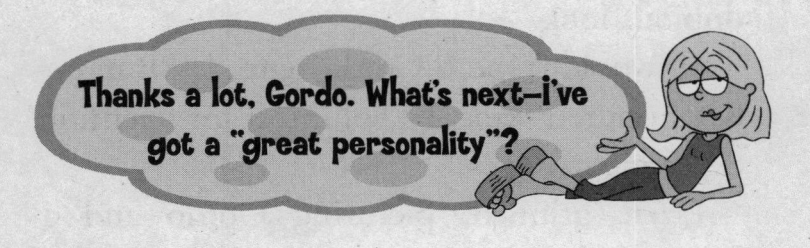

Thanks a lot, Gordo. What's next—I've got a "great personality"?

"Well, for once, being typical is finally paying off," Lizzie said.

"That's good. Milk it," said a loud voice behind them. Lizzie jumped back, startled.

"Whoa! Mr. Dig," Lizzie said, recovering. Mr. Dig was a substitute teacher who always seemed to have a gig at their school. He was a hip, young African American guy, and he usually came up with some pretty crazy projects for his classes. Today he was wearing a tie, which probably meant that he wasn't subbing in gym, although you never knew with Mr. Dig. "Where'd you come from?" Lizzie asked him.

"Well, my family's originally from Tobago, but I was born in East Lansing, Michigan." Mr. Dig grinned. "Go, Wolverines!"

Ohhh-kay, Lizzie thought. Whatever that means.

"So, you heard Lizzie is going to be a model?" Miranda asked.

"I did," Mr. Dig replied, nodding. "And I give her the same advice I gave supermodel Colette Romana."

Lizzie and her friends looked at one another. Who in the universe was Colette Romana?

"I told her, 'You have a natural gift. Share it with the world, and the world will love you,'" Mr. Dig said. He turned to Miranda. "Colette Romana. True story," he added, nodding with satisfaction.

Miranda uneasily adjusted the strap of her book bag. "Um . . . I've never heard of Colette Romana," she admitted.

"Well, that's because on her first photo shoot, in Nairobi, a zebra sat on her head and broke her face," Mr. Dig explained. He shook his head sadly. "Could've been famous. Tragic." He sighed and shivered at the thought.

Gordo spoke up. "Mr. Dig, I don't think you need to be famous to be happy."

"Oh, boy, please!" Mr. Dig scoffed. "You don't have to be *tall* to play in the NBA! You don't have to be *funny*-looking to be the Queen of England! You don't have to be seven hundred *pounds* to be a sumo wrestler!" He lifted his eyebrows. "But it helps."

Mr. Dig turned to Lizzie and pointed at her, a grim expression on his face. "Stay away from zebras," he advised seriously. Then he smiled. "Peace!" he chirped before flashing the peace sign and making his way down the hall.

"Shouldn't teachers be telling us that fame and money aren't important, and that we should focus on being good people?" Gordo asked, once Mr. Dig was out of earshot.

Lizzie pressed her lips together thoughtfully. Gordo was always going in for that

high-ideals kind of stuff. "He's just a substitute," Lizzie pointed out after a moment. "I guess he's allowed to tell us the truth."

They all shrugged and looked at one another blankly.

Teachers, Lizzie thought. Who can figure them out?

CHAPTER TWO

Matt looked around the store where his grandmother had purchased his gift certificate. It was called 2 Cool 4 U, and it had tons of neat gadgets, from camping gear to electronics. Matt was there with his parents and his best friend, Lanny.

"So, I can get anything I want with my gift certificate?" Matt asked eagerly. He was determined to find the hippest fifty-dollar item in the store—even if it took all day.

"As long as it doesn't produce flame," Mr. McGuire said, sounding tired.

"Or make loud noises," Mrs. McGuire added.

Mr. McGuire nodded. "Or hurt when I step on it."

Matt saluted. "Roger that." There had been a lot of Dad-gadget-stepping incidents lately. Matt guessed that meant a pocketknife was out of the question.

Matt grinned at the racks of neat gadgets. "Man, look at all this cool stuff. What should I get, Lanny?"

There was no response. Not unusual for Lanny. But when Matt looked around, he realized that his friend had disappeared. "Lanny?" Matt finally peered into the corner, where Lanny was sitting in a massive, brown leather massage chair. He had a remote control in his hand, and he was vibrating up and down with a huge grin on his face.

"Hey, that's a great idea," Matt said as he hurried over to the chair. "I've always wanted one of these." Matt picked up the price tag attached to the arm of the chair. But when he read the number on the tag, his mouth dropped open in shock. "Three thousand dollars?" he shouted. "Come on, Lanny. We better keep looking."

Lanny didn't move. Actually, he did move—he kept vibrating up and down. But he didn't get out of the massage chair.

"Lanny, come *on*," Matt said, grabbing his friend's arm.

Lanny frowned.

"Let's go, Lanny!" Matt complained. Lanny pounded on Matt's hand to make him let go. He did not want to leave that massage chair.

Matt finally gave up and went to explore the store himself. He found a weird personal massager shaped like a giant hammer. When

Matt pressed the ON button, the thing went crazy, nearly attacking him! Lanny jumped out of his chair to help, but even the two of them couldn't combat the out-of-control massager. Matt finally had to throw it on the ground and give it a good kick to get it to stop. He looked around the store to make sure that no salespeople had seen that. "Uh, let's go look at something else," Matt said quickly. Lanny nodded.

Meanwhile, Mr. McGuire tested out an aerodynamically designed bed, and Mrs. McGuire looked at an enlarging mirror. She inspected her teeth, which looked like golf balls thanks to the giant reflection in the mirror. Mrs. McGuire peered more closely. She had never noticed that the gaps between her teeth were so wide. . . .

Matt and Lanny went back to the massage chair and added a foot massager. That tickled

so much, they could barely get out of the chair. Finally, Lanny found something that was in their price range, but Matt wasn't really interested in an electronic tie organizer. Then they looked at a couple of chairs shaped like eggs.

"I shall call him . . . Mini-Me," Matt joked, holding his pinky to his lips.

Across the store, Lanny motioned for Matt to join him—he'd found a cool virtual-reality game. They spent about twenty minutes virtually kickboxing each other; then they got bored. Besides, the game cost more than a thousand dollars.

Matt took off his visor and sighed. He was beginning to think there wasn't anything in the store that he both wanted and could afford.

Suddenly, his eye fell on something across the store—a hammock that had its own

supports. That meant it could be used even in a backyard like the McGuires', which didn't have any trees. Matt hurried over to inspect it.

"Look, Lanny—it's perfect!" Matt said happily. Then he glanced at the price tag, and his grin disappeared. "'Sale, as is, seventy-five dollars,'" he read. Twenty-five dollars more than his gift certificate was worth.

Lanny stretched the hammock. Then he looked at Matt and nodded.

"Hey, that's right—" Matt said slowly, "—you're starting to earn money from your Web site."

Lanny grinned.

"Okay," Matt said. "We'll split it. My gift certificate, and you put up the rest. This is perfect." He grinned at the hammock, imagining long, lazy days hanging out in the backyard with a tropical drink. "Don't you think

so, Lanny?" Matt looked around. His friend had disappeared again. "Lanny?" Matt called. "Lanny?"

His friend was back in the massage chair. His father was asleep on the aerodynamic bed. And his mom was obsessing over her teeth. But Matt didn't care.

He had finally found the perfect birthday present. And it wasn't even his birthday.

CHAPTER THREE

"**T**hanks for coming tonight, everyone," said the stylish young African American woman behind the podium. Hip techno music was blasting through the store, and Lizzie was wearing a supercute plum-colored dress, which she would get to keep after the fashion show. She was way excited, but kind of nervous, too. So far, getting ready for the show had been lots of fun. The other models were really cool, and the hair and makeup

stylist had done a great job—Lizzie had never felt so glam. She couldn't wait to get out on the runway and strut her stuff.

Lizzie tried to just focus on the announcer's voice as she went on. "I'm Natasha O'Neal. *Teen Attitude* is very excited to present Stylin' 'N' Sassy. We've got some awesome young people backstage, and they're eager to get going."

Tell me about it, Lizzie thought as she straightened her skirt.

"So, let's give it up for them!" Natasha started clapping, and the audience let out a cheer. From her place behind the curtain, Lizzie could see her friends and family in the crowd. Gordo and Miranda had staked out the front row. And there were lots of other faces she recognized, too. It seemed like the whole school had come out to see the fashion show! Even Kate Sanders and her posse of the ultracool were there. Kate was sitting between

a popular girl named Jessica, whom Lizzie hardly knew, and—*sigh*—superhottie Ethan Craft.

Lizzie wasn't the first model out, so she watched the other girls as they walked down the runway. The ones who looked the best were the ones who seemed to be having a good time. I can do this, Lizzie told herself. I just have to remember to smile!

Finally, it was Lizzie's turn. She walked out onto the stage, and immediately felt everyone's eyes on her. Surprisingly, her nerves just evaporated! Lizzie felt terrific. She grinned and took her first turn, adding a little gesture with the straw bag she was carrying. This was fun!

Just as Lizzie walked off the stage, she overheard Jessica talking to Kate in the audience.

"Lizzie's pretty good," Jessica said.

Lizzie's grin got even wider.

"I could have done this if I hadn't had to go to a stupid funeral the day of tryouts," Kate griped.

"Lizzie! All *right*!" Ethan said with awe in his voice.

Kate narrowed her eyes in Lizzie's direction, but Lizzie didn't notice. She had already scurried backstage to change into her next outfit, which was a cute, green hippie-style blouse and skirt. A stylist ran in and changed her hairdo, then handed her a bouquet of flowers to carry. Before she knew it, Lizzie was back out onstage, striking poses and smiling. She couldn't help it—she was really enjoying herself!

When Lizzie came out in her next outfit— an orange flower print dress with a matching flower in her hair—she even gave Gordo and Miranda a little wave. They cheered wildly.

"Our little girl's really growing up," Mrs.

McGuire said wistfully to her husband as she watched Lizzie strike a kicky pose at the end of the runway.

"You know, honey, I have a new rule," Mr. McGuire said, leaning toward his wife. "Our little girl is not allowed to leave the house until she's twenty-five."

Mrs. McGuire shook her head and smiled.

"Let's give a big thank-you to all our beautiful models," Natasha said as the models joined hands and took a bow. Lizzie couldn't stop smiling as she trotted off the runway. I can't believe I just finished my first fashion show! Lizzie thought. That was such a blast!

Lizzie ran up to Gordo and Miranda. She was still wearing the orange dress and huge flower in her hair, but she didn't care—she wanted to see her best friends. They were waiting for her by the runway in the front of the store. "Oh, you guys!" Lizzie said giddily.

"Guys, listen! They're doing another show next week, and they want me to be in it!"

"That's incredible!" Miranda gushed.

"Check you out—you're going to be famous!" Gordo said proudly.

Lizzie giggled.

"Don't let all this go to your head, now," Gordo added, mock-seriously. He placed his hands over his heart. "Don't forget us little people when you're a big celebrity."

"Oh, I won't," Lizzie joked, giving her hair a toss. "Don't worry . . . um . . . um . . ." She snapped her fingers, as though her best friend's name had momentarily slipped her mind.

"Gordo," Gordo prompted.

"Gordo! Right!" Lizzie said with a laugh.

Miranda cracked up.

Just then, Lizzie noticed Ethan, Kate, and Jessica walking toward them.

"Lizzie," Ethan said, giving her a big smile, "All *right*!"

For a minute, it seemed like Ethan was about to stop and chat, but Kate swatted him on the back of the head and he kept walking.

"Hey, there you are!" Jessica said as she walked up to Lizzie. "We've been looking for you!"

Lizzie gave her a confused smile. Obviously, the "we" didn't include Kate, who was already walking away. And since when did Jessica want to talk to Lizzie? They hardly knew each other. Of course, Lizzie knew who *Jessica* was, even though they'd never really talked. She was one of the most popular girls in school.

"That was a bangin' show," Jessica said excitedly. "You really looked cool up there."

"Thanks," Lizzie said, shrugging shyly. She really had no idea what to say next. Luckily, Jessica took over.

"Listen, a bunch of us are getting together at my dad's club tomorrow afternoon," Jessica said. "We're going to go in the hot tub and watch the new Backstreet Boys DVD."

Miranda's mouth dropped open in shock. "But that's not even out yet," she said.

"My dad pulled some strings and got an advance copy," Jessica said. Her auburn hair was styled in a cute flip, and she shrugged it over her shoulders as she explained, "He's trying to buy me and my sister's affection."

"He's got mine," Miranda said enthusiastically.

Lizzie glanced at her friends. Jessica's offer sounded really cool. But Lizzie wanted her best friends to know that there was no way she was going to ditch them to hang with some popular people. Besides, Jessica just thinks I'm cool because I did some dumb fashion show, Lizzie thought. Gordo and

Miranda have been my friends for life. "Thanks," Lizzie told Jessica apologetically, "but it's just that Gordo and Miranda and I were planning on going to a movie tomorrow."

"They can come, too," Jessica offered, "if they want." She looked hesitantly at Miranda and Gordo, as though she wasn't sure that they would say yes.

"Oh, they want," Miranda assured her. "They want," she added through clenched teeth, staring at Lizzie.

"Let me get this straight," Gordo said to Lizzie. "Just because you did a fashion show, we're suddenly invited to a country club to hang out with all the popular kids that always ignored us before?"

Jessica looked at the floor, clearly embarrassed.

"We don't have to go if you don't want to, Gordo," Lizzie said in a low voice.

"Are you insane?" Gordo demanded. "I just wanted to get it *straight*. I've never been to a country club before. This is going to be awesome!"

Lizzie and Jessica grinned at each other. So the cool plan was on. And Gordo was right—it was going to be awesome!

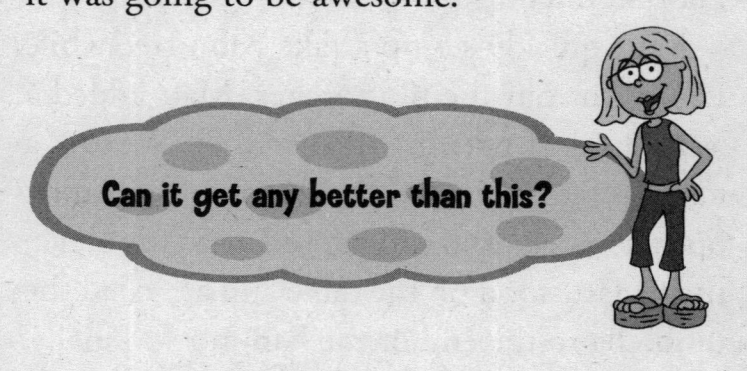

Can it get any better than this?

* * *

Matt and Lanny surveyed the green expanse of the McGuires' backyard.

"Are we ready?" Matt asked.

Lanny nodded.

Matt took a flying leap off the deck and ran

toward the pile of stuff he and Lanny had collected. Lanny had used some of his Web site money to buy a few "extras" to go with the hammock. They were determined to make the McGuire backyard the biggest paradise in the United States—not counting Hawaii, of course.

Matt quickly set up a fake palm tree while Lanny got out the tiki torches. Matt added a large bird-of-paradise plant, then set up a table to go next to the hammock. Lanny opened a giant multicolored sun umbrella; then Matt stood on the table and attached the umbrella to the end of the hammock. Finally, everything was almost ready. The friends shook hands, and Matt ran to the kitchen to get their drinks. Lanny had even bought two special plastic cups—one shaped like a pineapple for Matt, and one shaped like a coconut for himself—which Matt filled

with cola and topped with tiny umbrellas.

Matt joined Lanny outside, and together they surveyed the scene. There was no doubt about it—the hammock looked good.

"This is the life," Matt said as he and Lanny crawled onto the hammock. They spread out and clinked their glasses.

Suddenly, there was a loud tearing noise— *riiip!*—as the hammock tore in half!

"Arg!" Matt cried. Cola flew everywhere as he and Lanny tumbled to the ground. The hammock was ruined, not to mention the fact that their very expensive backyard paradise was toast. But Matt had another problem.

"Lanny . . ." Matt said with a groan, "you're squishing me."

"Look at all this shrimp toast!" Gordo said as a waiter held out a silver platter. Gordo reached out of the hot tub, grabbed a large

ast, and popped a huge chunk of it mouth.

zie and Miranda gave each other ssed-out looks. Gordo was dropping pieces of shrimp toast into the hot tub! Not to mention the fact that he was wearing his father's sunglasses, which were about five sizes too big. With his hair slicked back from the pool, Gordo looked like some weird bug attacking a crumb. "Oh, that's good shrimp toast," he said, his mouth full. "You guys gonna have some shrimp toast? I'm gonna have some more shrimp toast." He tore off another piece of his toast and motioned to the waiter for more.

"Uh. No thanks, Gordo," Lizzie said quickly. She eyed him as he dropped more crumbs into the hot tub. This was getting downright disgusting. "Hey. You guys want to go get something to drink?" she said quickly.

"Try the iced tea," Gordo advised, still chewing. "It's got a sprig of mint in it. It's very refreshing." Gordo had spent most of the day taking advantage of everything the country club had to offer, from the complimentary golf balls to the scented towels. He seemed amazed that everything there was free. Lizzie suspected that he would move into the club permanently, if given half a chance.

"Nothing for me, thanks," Jessica said.

"Be back in a minute," Miranda said as she and Lizzie climbed out of the hot tub. "This is massive," Miranda whispered to Lizzie as they headed to the poolside snack bar. "You should've been a model years ago."

"Yeah," Lizzie agreed. "Then maybe for the fifth-grade holiday pageant, Mrs. Thalheimer would've let me play the Snow Princess, not a sheep."

Well, who's laughing now, Mrs. i-Got-Axed-for-Stealing-Supplies-and-Now-i-Sell-Hot-Dogs-in-Front-of-Lumber-for-Less? Hmm? Who's laughing now?!

Just then, the two girls at the front of the snack bar line got their drinks and turned around. *Ugh.* One of them was Kate. Lizzie waited to hear one of her ex-friend's usual disses, but instead, Kate turned to the girl she was with and started giggling like crazy.

"Lizzie," Kate said, grinning as though Lizzie were her best friend in the world. "What's this I hear about you and *Teen Attitude* magazine?"

"Oh, they called me last night after the

fashion show and wanted me to do some photo shoots for them," Lizzie said nonchalantly. She inspected her fingernails, as though this wasn't the most exciting thing that had ever happened to her.

"We heard you're going to be on the cover." Kate gushed. "Wow."

"That's right, wow," Miranda snapped. "Lizzie's going to be famous."

"What kind of outfits do you get to wear?" Kate wanted to know. "Where's the photo shoot?"

"Um, Lizzie doesn't want to answer questions all day long," Miranda said harshly. "She's just looking for a little quiet time."

"Oh, okay, okay." Kate backed away, clearly not wanting to bother the "star."

"I am?" Lizzie asked. She stared at Miranda. Since when had her friend started handling people for her?

"You are," Miranda said, steering Lizzie toward the snack bar as Kate scurried off. Miranda leaned against the snack bar. "Why don't you go back to the hot tub," she suggested. "I'll get your drink. What do you want?"

Lizzie shrugged. "Water."

"What kind?" Miranda asked.

Lizzie frowned, confused. "The, uh . . . the wet kind."

"They have sparkling Italian, French, and Swiss," Miranda listed, "artesian from the Julian Alps in Slovenia, deep-spring from Utah—"

Lizzie shook her head—Miranda's list was making her dizzy. Who knew there were that many kinds of water in the world? "Maybe I'll just have some tea."

"Oh! They have mango, raspberry, lemon, spearmint mist, cinnamon . . ." Miranda went

on and on. Clearly, there was no such thing as an easy drink order at this country club. When Miranda got to the cherry-infused variety, Lizzie just gave up and let her friend make the decision. It was easier than listening to her endless lists!

Besides, who really cares about all of that stuff, anyway? Lizzie wondered as the guy behind the snack bar poured her drink. A drink is a drink.

I'll just let Miranda handle it, Lizzie decided.

"Thanks, Dad," Jessica said as an older man in tennis whites handed her a tropical-looking drink.

"I've known Lizzie my entire life," Gordo said as he relaxed in the hot tub. "I always knew she'd be discovered—that's why I put her in all my movies. You know, if you want, I could come over sometime, show 'em to you."

Jessica leaned forward eagerly. "Would Lizzie come?" she asked.

"Yes," Gordo said, nodding. "Yes, yes she would."

"Great," Jessica said with a bright smile. "How about next Sunday?"

Just then, Lizzie and Miranda stepped back into the hot tub. Lizzie wasn't sure what her drink was. All she knew was that it was green and it tasted good. Miranda's drink was red. Strawberry something—Lizzie'd had a sip. She had to hand it to her friend—Miranda sure knew how to place a drink order.

"Lizzie—" Gordo said as Lizzie sat down, balancing her drink carefully, "next Sunday, we're all going to go to Jessica's house and watch movies. She has HDTV and surround sound."

"Oh, I can't," Lizzie said, disappointed. "That's when my next fashion show is."

"Oh, that's in the afternoon," Miranda pointed out. "You're free by seven."

"We'll do it at seven," Gordo said happily.

"Great." Jessica grinned.

"Great." Gordo agreed.

"Great." Miranda chimed in.

"Wait," Lizzie said, hesitating.

"What?" Gordo asked.

Maybe i don't want to spend all my time hanging out with cool kids in hot tubs!

What, am I delirious? Lizzie wondered. I must be cracking up. That thought didn't even make sense! Lizzie nodded. "Sunday at seven sounds good."

"Perfect," Miranda said. "And Saturday night we could all go dancing."

"Coolie." Jessica smiled. "The Shango Tango is hard to get into," she said, naming the coolest teen club in town, "but if we're with Lizzie, that shouldn't be a problem." Jessica smiled at Miranda, who smiled at Gordo. Everyone was smiling.

Everyone except Lizzie.

Why does this feel so weird? Lizzie wondered as she took a sip of her delicious drink. Shouldn't I just relax and have fun? She sighed.

Since when did having fun seem like such hard work?

CHAPTER FOUR

The next Monday, as Lizzie walked down the school stairs toward her locker, she noticed that a girl was staring at her. Lizzie frowned, then saw that a guy was staring at her, too. What is the deal? Lizzie wondered. Do I have something on my face? When she hit the last step, she turned and looked up the stairs. Everyone had stopped walking and was looking at her. It sent a little creepy chill down her spine. Lizzie was about to ask

whether she had something horrible stuck in her hair when she heard a familiar voice.

"Hey, Lizzie!" Kate said as she rushed up to her. "That is a great blouse."

"Oh, thanks." Lizzie looked down at the purple shirt she was wearing. It had sequins on it and was one of her favorites.

"And your earrings match your eyes," Kate went on.

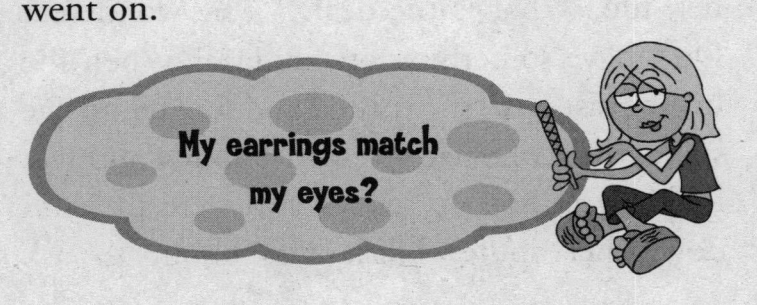

Lizzie imagined two brown eyeballs dangling from her earlobes. That was definitely one of the weirder compliments she'd ever gotten.

"And your shoes are way cool, too," Kate added.

Lizzie stared down at the scuffed black sneakers she was wearing. "Thanks."

i need rubber boots with all the manure she's shoveling.

Lizzie wondered how many fake compliments she'd have to suffer through before Kate got to the point.

"So, I'll see you at the Shango Tango on Saturday?" Kate asked hopefully.

Lizzie gave Kate a tight smile. So that was it. Kate wanted to hang out with Lizzie so that she could get into the club this weekend. "Yeah," Lizzie said unenthusiastically. "Can't wait."

Kate giggled, clapped her hands, and hurried away. Lizzie sighed. Is the price of popularity really this high? Lizzie wondered. She guessed it was.

Suddenly, Lizzie saw a familiar figure in front of her. It was Ethan. He had his back to her and was chatting with a friend.

Okay, here's your chance, Lizzie told herself. Ethan had seemed really impressed by her at the fashion show. Maybe now I can talk to him without making a fool of myself, Lizzie thought, for once. She straightened her blouse.

"Hey, Ethan!" Lizzie chirped.

Ethan whirled. When he saw Lizzie, his jaw

dropped. "Me?" he said uncertainly. "Um . . . hi." He looked at the floor.

"Um." Lizzie wasn't sure what to say next. Ethan was acting kind of shy for some reason. "So . . . what did you think of the English test?" Lizzie asked.

"I don't know," Ethan said haltingly. "What did *you* think?"

"Oh, I thought it was really hard." Lizzie laughed self-consciously.

"Yeah, yeah, it was hard," Ethan agreed. "It was, it was really hard."

Lizzie frowned. Ethan was squirming like a worm on a hook. "Are you okay?" Lizzie asked.

"I don't know, am I?" Ethan babbled. He looked everywhere but at Lizzie—it was almost as if he were too nervous to face her, or something. "I mean . . . I . . . you—I gotta go." Ethan scrambled away.

Wow, Lizzie thought. Things are getting way out of hand.

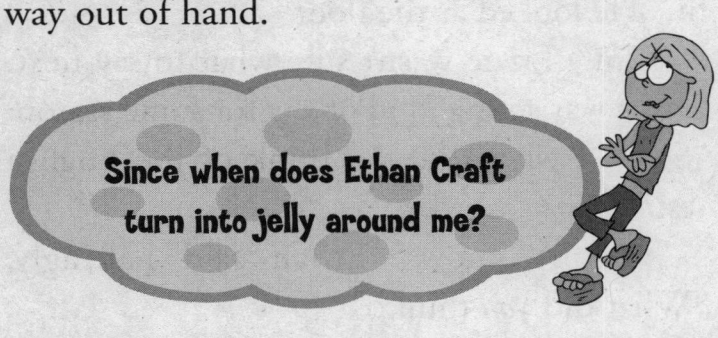

Since when does Ethan Craft turn into jelly around me?

This would be cool if it weren't so creepy, Lizzie thought as she yanked open her locker and put her supplies inside. Suddenly, she got a weird feeling—like all of the hair on the back of her head was standing on end. She turned and saw this little nerd from the Chess Club gaping at her, his jaw hanging open. "Ugh!" Lizzie said, slamming her locker.

Miranda walked up and shoved the kid away. "Why don't you take a picture?" she shouted after him. "It'll last longer."

Gordo stared after the kid, shaking his

head, as the little nerd scampered down the hall in embarrassment.

"I'm glad you guys are here," Lizzie said, breathing a sigh of relief. "This modeling thing is starting to make everyone all freaky."

Gordo raised his eyebrows. "I'm sure not everyone's acting freaky," he said doubtfully.

"Kate Sanders is complimenting me," Lizzie said, ticking the items off on her fingers. "Ethan Craft is all of a sudden like a drooling chimp. Everyone's acting all different ever since I became a 'celebrity.'" Lizzie put finger quotes around the word "celebrity" and rolled her eyes.

"Well, would you rather Kate be mean to you, like usual?" Miranda asked.

"No." Lizzie scoffed. "But it's just so . . . weird. People who never liked me before want to be my best friend now."

"Who cares?" Miranda demanded. "We're popular now."

Lizzie frowned. "We?" she repeated.

"You," Miranda amended. "*You* are popular."

She said "we." i was right here—i heard her.

Lizzie narrowed her eyes. Wait a minute. Was it possible that her own best friend was using her, too—using her to get popular?

"You *are* popular," Gordo pointed out. "In fact, Whitney Nussbaum wants us to go to her Bat Mitzvah Saturday." He lifted his eyebrows. "They're giving away cell phones as party favors."

"I can't," Lizzie said irritably. "I can't go to the Shango Tango Saturday night and a Bat Mitzvah during the day. I have a book report due on *Lord of the Flies.*"

"I'll write that for you," Gordo offered.

Lizzie's eyes grew round. "You think doing other people's homework is wrong," she said, pointing at Gordo. "I've asked you, like, a million times."

"These are special circumstances," Gordo explained smoothly. "You got a lot on your plate. I'll write the report."

"Problem solved," Miranda said cheerily. "See ya." She and Gordo walked off.

Problem not solved! Problem huge! My friends are turning into freaks!

Lizzie stared after her friends, who were talking as they strode down the hall together. Probably planning all of my future activities, Lizzie thought miserably. Like, do I have any spare time at 4:30 A.M. next Tuesday? *Grrrrr.*

This is horrible. Gordo and Miranda aren't my friends anymore. They're . . . my "people."

CHAPTER FIVE

As Lizzie walked down the hall toward her next class, she noticed some major weirdness going on. The hall, which normally would have been full of kids laughing and talking at the level usually reserved for rock concerts, was deathly quiet. Every single person was staring at her. It reminded her of a fun house she'd gone to when she was six years old, where there were all of these old paintings on

the walls that followed you with their eyes. It was majorly freakish. Mr. McGuire had to carry Lizzie out of there, screaming, and she only stopped crying when he promised that they could go home and never come back. And now, the same thing was happening at her own junior high school!

Stop staring at me. I am not a celebrity! I am a human being!

Finally, Lizzie couldn't take it anymore. She ducked into the nearest empty classroom and slammed the door. Then she peered out into the hall from a little glass window in the door. Good—no one had followed her. Okay, here's the plan, Lizzie told herself as she covered her eyes and backed into the room: when the bell

rings and the hall clears, I dash to geometry and sneak in the back. . . .

"Hey, how you doing?" said a cheery voice behind Lizzie.

"Wah!" Lizzie whirled around, uncovering her eyes.

"Aw, I'm sorry. Did I startle you?" Mr. Dig asked. He was seated at a heavy teacher's desk. The chalkboard behind him was filled with the names of foreign countries.

"No." Lizzie shook her head. "It's just—"

Suddenly, there was a burst of light. Lizzie's jaw dropped open. Mr. Dig had just taken an instant photograph of her!

"Thanks," Mr. Dig said, plucking the photo from the front of the camera. "My nephew didn't believe I know the new *Teen Attitude* girl."

"Great," Lizzie said sarcastically. "Now you're acting like everyone else."

"What? Other people are selling your picture to my nephew?" Mr. Dig asked.

Lizzie's eyebrows drew together. "You're selling my picture to your nephew?" She couldn't believe this!

Flash! The flashbulb popped again as Mr. Dig took another candid shot. "I got a niece, too." He waved the photo in the air, then frowned. "What's bugging you?"

Lizzie folded her arms across her chest. "Everybody's acting all weird," she said. "Gordo's using me to get invited places, and Miranda's scheduling me. I can't take it anymore."

"Ahhh," Mr. Dig said as though he understood everything perfectly. "I don't know who those people are."

Lizzie rolled her eyes. "Oh, well, they're supposed to be my friends. But ever since this modeling thing, they've been treating me completely different." She sighed.

"Ah! I get it," Mr. Dig said. "You don't want them acting like your posse."

"Right!" Lizzie said, glad that someone finally understood how she felt. "So . . ." she asked slowly, "what do I do?"

"Treat 'em like your posse," Mr. Dig said simply.

Lizzie gave him a dubious look. Why do I even bother asking teachers for advice on anything? she wondered.

"Look, you're a celebrity now," Mr. Dig explained. "It's human nature for them to treat you differently. If you want them to go back to being your friends, you have to show them why they shouldn't act like miserable, groveling suck-up dogs."

i like substitutes. They teach you useful stuff.

Lizzie lifted her eyebrows. Actually, Mr. Dig had a seriously good point. "So, as a teacher, you're telling me to treat my friends like dirt?"

"No, I'm telling you as a buddy," Mr. Dig replied. "As a *teacher*, I'm telling you that France exports aerospace products, and Italy is shaped like a boot."

Lizzie bit her lip. Sometimes Mr. Dig made no sense. Like now.

"I'm teaching geography this week," Mr. Dig explained. "I get in trouble if I deviate from the lesson plan." He picked up his camera again and aimed it at Lizzie. "Say, '*fromage*,'" he chirped.

Lizzie blinked as the flashbulb went off again. But for once, she didn't really mind. A couple of pictures was a small price to pay if it meant that she just might be able to get her friends back.

* * *

"Let me do the talking, okay, Lanny?" Matt said as he and Lanny walked into 2 Cool 4 U, carrying the long box in which the broken hammock had been packed. They strode up to a youngish salesman with a goatee who was busy testing a treadmill.

"Matt, I'll handle it," Mr. McGuire said as he walked up behind his son and put a hand on his shoulder. "Excuse me," Mr. McGuire said to the salesman.

The salesman ignored him.

Mr. McGuire tried again. "Excuse me."

The salesman finally looked up. "I'm exercising," he snapped as he continued his power walk. "Twenty more minutes."

Mr. McGuire laughed uncomfortably. "Um, my son bought this hammock, and when we got it home, it ripped in half," he said politely. "We'd like a refund."

"Oh, I getcha," the salesman said with a smile. Then his expression darkened. "No."

Mr. McGuire planted his hands on his hips. "Excuse me?"

"No returns on sale items," the salesman barked.

"But it was ripped!" Matt protested.

"Yeah, it's defective," Mr. McGuire agreed.

Lanny nodded.

"So he shouldn't have bought it," the salesman said snidely. "Look, I told you, old-timer, I'm exercising." The salesman turned up one of the knobs on the treadmill.

"That's it," Matt said as he and Lanny dropped the box. "Get tough with him, Lanny."

Lanny flexed his muscles and began to breathe like an angry bull.

The salesman rolled his eyes.

Mr. McGuire leaned toward the boys. "Matt,

I'm going to get the manager." He turned to Lanny, who was still doing his flared-nostrils routine. "Thanks." Mr. McGuire patted Lanny's shoulder.

Matt finally realized that Lanny's intimidation tactics weren't working, so he scanned the store for another solution. He found a roll of duct tape lying on a shelf.

"Hey," Matt said brightly, "maybe we can fix the hammock." He looked at the salesman and held up the roll of tape. "Excuse me, sir, do you think we could use this tape to fix the hammock?"

"I'd rather use it to tape up your mouth," the salesman said sarcastically.

"Ha-ha, that's a good one," Matt said in his best I'm-not-going-to-admit-you're-a-jerk voice. "Very interesting." His eyes clouded over. "But I've got a better idea." Quickly, Matt darted toward the rail of the treadmill and

taped the salesman's wrist to it. "Help me, Lanny!" he cried as he passed the roll to Lanny, who tied up the salesman's other wrist. Matt grinned devilishly. "Lanny, do you suppose this treadmill goes faster?"

The salesman was still trying to figure out what had just happened as Lanny pressed a button on the treadmill. Suddenly, the salesman had stopped power walking, and was doing some serious power running!

"Hey! What are you doing?" the salesman demanded.

"Why, it does." Matt grinned, clearly delighted, and pressed the button again.

"Turn this thing off!" the salesman cried. Now his feet were just a blur as they moved to keep up with the treadmill. "Hey!"

"Lanny," Matt commanded, "tickle him."

Lanny reached for the salesman, his fingers wriggling.

"No! No!" the salesman cried, alternately screaming and laughing as Lanny tickled him. "Okay! Get a new hammock! Get a new one!"

Matt gave the salesman his most sarcastic grin. "Have fun exercising!"

"Uh, Lizzie?" Miranda called as she peered into the McGuires' front door. "Where are you?"

"I'm out back!" Lizzie shouted.

Gordo followed Miranda inside and shut the door. Then they walked through the house and out to the rear deck, where Lizzie was lying on a lounge chair, reading a fashion magazine and sipping a tropical drink. She was wearing pink sunglasses, an enormous fabric rose in her hair, and a long sheer robe trimmed with turquoise feathers. Her hair was perfectly coiffed, and she had on pale blue eye shadow that matched her nail polish.

Miranda and Gordo stood by the lounge chair.

Commence "Operation Superstar Brat."

"Yeah. Did you bring the jelly beans like I wanted?" Lizzie asked in a bored voice, not bothering to look up from her magazine. She flipped a page noisily.

"Uh," Miranda said, glancing at Gordo, "you didn't ask for any jelly beans."

"What—I have to *ask* now?" Lizzie slammed down her magazine. "There's some in the kitchen. Could you go get me some?"

"Uh, sure." Miranda scratched her head, clearly confused, but she headed into the kitchen obediently.

Lizzie folded her arms across her chest and

pursed her lips. "Where's the book report?" she asked Gordo.

"Hot off the printer," Gordo said as he handed it over.

Lizzie flipped the title page and read the first sentence. She scoffed. "No, no, no," she said, giving Gordo a snide glance. "Not good enough." Lizzie took the book report and blew her nose all over it, then crumpled it up and tossed it aside. "Do it over," she commanded.

"But I spent three hours on it," Gordo protested, staring at the crumpled mess on the ground.

"So, spend four," Lizzie said dismissively. She waved her hand in a vague gesture. "Make it more . . . fun."

"Fun?" Gordo repeated. "*Lord of the Flies* is about shipwrecked children eating one another."

Lizzie rolled her eyes. "That doesn't mean it has to be a drag." She pointed a blue fingernail at him. "Do it again, or you're not coming to Shango Tango with me tonight."

"Here," Miranda said as she handed Lizzie a bowl of jelly beans.

"Eeew." Lizzie frowned. "You didn't pick the green ones out."

"I didn't know I was supposed to," Miranda said as she took the bowl back from Lizzie.

"I don't need excuses," Lizzie snapped, as she ripped off her pink sunglasses and stood up. "What do I need you guys around for, if you can't do anything right? You want to keep messing up?" Lizzie's voice rose. "You want to keep acting like untrained dogs? Fine! Bark!" Lizzie was practically shouting now. "Go ahead—bark like dogs!"

"You're . . . joking, right?" Gordo said.

"You want to go to Whitney Nussbaum's Bat Mitzvah with me?" Lizzie asked. "Start barking." She waited. "*I said bark!*" Lizzie hollered.

Miranda stared at Gordo. "Woof," he said finally.

"Woof, woof," Miranda joined in, unenthusiastically. "Grr."

"That is pathetic," Lizzie said, gesturing impatiently with her sunglasses. "I don't know why I've been wasting my time with you guys."

Miranda and Gordo gaped at her in shock.

"I'm going to go find better people to hang out with!" Lizzie shoved them out of the way. "Move!" She commanded. Gordo and Miranda stumbled aside as Lizzie stomped into the kitchen.

Miranda and Gordo stared at each other, speechless.

Lizzie waited a moment, then walked slowly back outside. "See, wasn't that horrible?" she asked gently.

"Um, yeah," Miranda said.

"But you got my point, right?" Lizzie asked.

"That you've totally snapped your twig?" Gordo suggested.

"No," Lizzie said, shaking her head. "That you guys have changed."

"We haven't changed," Gordo insisted.

"Gordo! You let me blow my nose on your book report!" Lizzie pointed to the crumpled heap on the ground. "And, Miranda, you let me boss you around. Just because I'm 'becoming famous.'" Lizzie rolled her eyes.

Gordo and Miranda were silent for a little while.

"I guess I did get a little caught up with the

whole country-club/hot-tub stuff," Gordo admitted finally.

"Yeah," Lizzie said with a shrug, "but it's not worth you guys treating me differently. I need you guys to be my friends." She shook her head. "Not my posse."

"I guess I could go back to refusing to help you with your homework," Gordo offered.

"And I can tell you when your clothes make you look dorky and your hair looks like an ostrich," Miranda added.

Relieved, Lizzie smiled. "Thanks."

"Like now, for instance," Miranda said, eyeing the feathers on Lizzie's gown. "You look like you're molting."

Lizzie was glad that her friends finally understood where she was coming from. But she knew they weren't going to like what she had to say next. "Well, see, the thing is,"

Lizzie looked at the ground, "everybody else is still treating me differently. So I've got to stop being a model."

Gordo sighed. "Bye-bye, shrimp toast," he said miserably.

"And there's one more problem," Lizzie went on. "I've got a contract with *Teen Attitude*."

Everyone was silent for a moment.

"That's not a problem," Miranda said finally, smiling confidently. "All you have to do is *stink* at being a model."

Gordo looked at her and nodded.

Lizzie grinned at her friends. They were finally, really, truly back!

"Cheyenne Keegan in Lorenzo's new casual collection," Natasha announced into the microphone at the next *Teen Attitude* fashion show as a model took a turn in a short, lavender dress. The usual techno beat was blasting

away in the background, and nobody noticed as Gordo walked up to the soundboard with a Walkman and an adapter.

"And now, Lizzie McGuire in Andrea Taylor's new evening wear, Elegance in Ivory," Natasha went on as the audience applauded.

Quickly, Gordo attached one of the wires to the soundboard and pressed the PLAY button. Square-dancing music sounded through the store as Lizzie leaped onstage in a pair of off-white long johns. Actually, the long johns *used* to be white—they just looked off-white because they hadn't been washed in about three years, and they were ripped at the knee and armpit. Her front two teeth had been blackened out, and, as a bold accessory, she carried an enormous turkey leg. After ripping off a huge hunk of turkey, she began to sloppily chew.

There was a spattering of confused

applause from the audience. Everyone looked at one another, befuddled.

Okay, Lizzie thought as she took her first turn, maybe they think this is avant-garde fashion. I guess I'll have to be an even lousier model. Her ratted hair splayed wildly as she spun around, and Lizzie scratched her armpit. Then, for added effect, she turned and scratched her butt. Ah, yes, Lizzie thought as she slouched up the runway, nothing but elegance in ivory.

Gordo was laughing his head off from his place at the soundboard. He switched the music to a tuba solo as Lizzie took another stroll down the runway, tossing her turkey leg in Kate's lap as she went.

"Eek!" Kate shrieked as she slapped the turkey leg away.

Lizzie continued to clump down the catwalk, taking enormous, graceless steps.

Finally, she tripped over the *Teen Attitude* YOU TODAY sign, knocking it over. Lizzie recovered and grinned, showing off her blackened teeth.

"Way to go, graceful," Miranda called from the audience.

"Are you talkin' to me?" Lizzie demanded. "Who do you think you are?"

"Not a dorko, like you," Miranda replied, just as they had rehearsed in the McGuires' backyard the day before.

"I don't *think* so. . . ." Lizzie jumped from the runway and knocked Miranda out of her chair.

Gordo switched the music to some frantic silent-movie-style piano music as Lizzie and Miranda rolled around on the floor in a "catfight." The audience murmured in fright and cleared out of the store as the girls knocked over a rack of clothing.

"Lizzie, stop it!" Natasha cried, running over.

Lizzie and Miranda kept on clawing at each other. They had both agreed that they wouldn't stop until they got what they wanted.

"Stop it!" Natasha repeated, leaning over the girls from the runway. "That's it," she said finally, "there is no room for you at *Teen Attitude*." Natasha tossed her long black hair and stalked off.

Bingo! Lizzie and Miranda stopped fighting and grinned at each other. So Lizzie wasn't a model anymore. They'd done it!

The next afternoon, Lizzie, Miranda, and Gordo were lounging on chairs in the McGuires' backyard, each reading something different. Lizzie had a magazine, Miranda had a book, and Gordo had some technical manual on how to build rockets.

"Hey, Miranda," Lizzie said as she flipped through her magazine, "you wanna go get me some hot chocolate?"

"Get it yourself," Miranda said, not even glancing up from her book.

"How about you, Gordo?" Lizzie suggested, turning to her other friend.

"*Pfft!*" was Gordo's reply.

My friends are back!

"I'll go get it myself," Lizzie said with a laugh as she put down her magazine and hauled herself out of her chair.

"Could you, uh, bring me some?" Gordo called as she headed into the kitchen.

Lizzie glanced over her shoulder. "*Pfft!*" she said.

Gordo laughed.

Hey, Lizzie thought as she grinned to herself, what did he expect?

That's what friends are for.

Lizzie McGUiRE

PART TWO

CHAPTER ONE

"**B**iology," Gordo moaned as he walked up to Lizzie and Miranda's table on the lunch patio. Lizzie had to bite her lip to keep from laughing at his miserable state. Gordo was more loaded with books than the Library of Congress.

"Geology. World History. Intermediate Algebra." He shook his head as he plunked the pile of books on the table.

"Thanks, but we're trying to eat," Miranda said, eyeing the books with distaste. She

shoved her plate a little farther away from the offending books.

"Eat?" Gordo replied. "How can you eat when there's so much homework to do? Who has *time* to eat when there's so much home- work to do? And reading . . . and reports. Who knew that eighth grade was going to be so difficult?" He glanced at his pile of books with a look of horror.

Yikes, Lizzie thought. Gordo loves school. If he thinks there's too much work, you know it has to be true. And it's only the first week! Still, she wasn't going to let Gordo's attitude get her down. She was an eighth grader now—and it was her time to shine.

"Tell me about it," Miranda agreed with Gordo, rolling her eyes. "I had to get up in front of my French class today and conjugate a verb." She threw up her hands. "I don't even know how to do that in English!"

"Come on, you guys," Lizzie said brightly. "Being in eighth grade rocks."

"Igneous or sedimentary?" Gordo asked, holding up his geology book.

"I'm serious," Lizzie said. "We have experience now. There is an entire grade younger than us trying to figure out what we already know. But we are eighth graders now." She clenched her fist in triumph. "Eighth graders!"

Miranda and Gordo just stared at her.

Okay, guess i'll have to spell it out for them.

"Look at them," Lizzie said, pulling herself out of her chair and gesturing toward a line of frightened-looking seventh graders. They

were all clutching their notebooks to their chests and peering around timidly. "So young," Lizzie went on. "Scared. Nervous. And look at us"—she folded her arms across her chest securely—"older . . . wiser . . . *confident*." Lizzie looked down at her peasant blouse and denim skirt. Her hair was curled and she was wearing a slim, sparkly headband. And we're *definitely* more fashionable, she added mentally.

Miranda lifted her eyebrows so that they disappeared beneath the clean line of her dark bangs. "I'm sorry, did you just call yourself confident?" She sounded amused. Lizzie was pretty famous for her insecurities.

"It is kind of nice to walk down the hall and know where I'm going," Gordo admitted.

Miranda cocked her head. "And I guess it's kind of cool knowing which teachers to avoid," she added.

"Exactly!" Lizzie grinned. That's more like it! she thought. So far, week one of eighth grade had been a real boost to Lizzie's ego. Just knowing that there were other kids in the school who were more clueless than she was made her feel better about herself.

Seventh grade. Been there, done that. Outgrew the T-shirt and donated it to charity.

Lizzie planted her hands on her hips. "This year, it's about giving back," she declared.

"Giving back?" Miranda repeated.

"Yeah," Lizzie said. "Sharing what we know. I met this girl . . . she's a sevie and—"

Miranda and Gordo gaped at her with looks of utter confusion.

"You know," Lizzie said, sighing impatiently, "a seventh grader."

"Oh, a seventh grader. Right. Yeah." Gordo said quickly, as though he had been "down with the lingo" all along.

"Yeah. So. She kind of reminds me of me when I was her age," Lizzie explained. "You know, a little self-conscious, kind of shy. Ooh, there she is." Lizzie waved to a timid-looking girl across the lunch patio.

The girl waved back and smiled shyly. She had long, limp dark hair, and wore a plain T-shirt and jeans.

I just can't wait to mold her sense of style, Lizzie thought, imagining how her friend would look with a makeover. "If I had someone older a year ago to help me, I could've avoided some serious fashion don'ts," Lizzie said. She shuddered, remembering the brown plaid sweater she'd worn with the leopard-

print pants and a bright purple flower in her hair. Not to mention the '80s Blossom-style hair and ugly patchwork shirt she'd loved until Kate had started calling her Little Orphan Lizzie.

"Congratulations, Lizzie," Gordo said. "It's nice to see you being so altruistic."

"French is hard enough, Gordo," Miranda complained, rolling her eyes at Gordo's vocabulary. "Translation, please?"

"It's just nice to see her being so helpful, that's all," Gordo explained.

Lizzie smiled and shrugged.

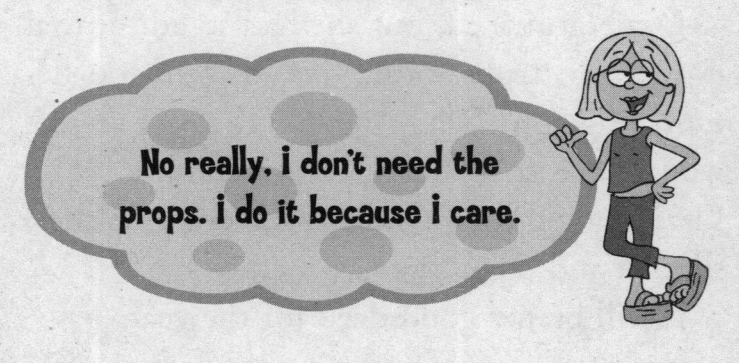

No really, i don't need the props. i do it because i care.

Just then, Lizzie's seventh-grade friend, Andie Robinson, got up from her seat. She took three steps, then tripped, dropping all of her books and notebooks. Half the lunch patio cracked up. Andie looked up at Lizzie. Lizzie gave her a friendly wave.

"You're right," Gordo observed. "She *is* like you."

"Exactly like you," Miranda said wryly.

Hey!

Lizzie grimaced, but she had to admit that it was the truth. Still, that only made her more eager to help Andie. I'll do it so she won't have to suffer the humiliation I did, Lizzie thought, remembering every time she'd slipped and fallen the year before.

It will be my good deed for the year.

Lizzie walked up to her new locker on the eighth-grade hall and tried to pry it open. No good. So far, this locker was about as friendly as her last one had been—in other words, not at all. Lizzie spun the combination again and then yanked on the door. It didn't budge, so she slammed it and yanked harder. Suddenly, it flew open, whacking her in the face.

"Ugh!" Lizzie cried as she fell flat on her back in the hallway.

Star light, star bright . . . Why does this keep happening to me?

Why do I always get stuck with the killer attack-locker that knows just when to

pounce? Lizzie wondered as she tried to blink the flashing lights out of her eyes.

Two Andies peered down at Lizzie. "Lizzie, are you okay?" they both asked.

Lizzie rubbed her eyes. "You're a twin?" she asked. The two Andies merged into one as the seventh grader reached out and helped Lizzie to her feet.

"I just wanted to thank you for your advice before," Andie said, smiling happily. "I tied up my P.E. T-shirt like you suggested, and before I knew it, everybody was doing it." Her eyes sparkled as she gazed at Lizzie admiringly.

Lizzie smiled, glad that her first piece of advice had turned out so well for Andie.

Just then, a familiar snooty voice sounded from down the hall. "You know what they say . . ." Kate Sanders strutted down the hall, her posse trailing behind her like fashionable

ducklings. "You can take the girl out of seventh grade, but you can't take seventh grade out of the girl. Like, who still hangs around with," she sneered at Andie, "sevies?" Kate rolled her eyes and stalked off.

"Is that Kate Sanders?" Andie asked once Kate was out of earshot. "I hear she's really mean." She winced. "Unless of course, you guys are friends," she added quickly, with a nervous laugh. "Then I'm sure she's really nice."

"Well," Lizzie said slowly, "let's just say Kate and I have a very interesting relationship." She smiled at the understatement.

Andie nodded.

Suddenly, Lizzie's eye fell on something tall, dark blond, and gorgeous headed her way. It was Ethan Craft, who was, unbelievably, even hotter than he had been last year. Even his hair was glossier—which Lizzie hadn't realized was possible.

"Hey, Ethan," Lizzie said brightly.

"Lizzie." Ethan leaned in toward her. "Looking good this year," he said without breaking his stride.

"Right back at you," Lizzie called smoothly as Ethan headed toward his locker.

Did I just say that to Ethan Craft? This really is a new me.

"You actually know him?" Andie asked, clearly impressed.

"Yeah, kind of," Lizzie said with a grin. She turned to her locker and grabbed her books before the metal door had time to attack her again.

"He's the boy I was going to ask you

about," Andie said dreamily. "I totally have a crush." She looked up at the ceiling and sighed. "Can't help it."

"Yeah," Lizzie said as she and Andie started down the hall. "Join the club. Ethan kind of has that effect on people." She grinned, seeing how blissed out Andie was over Ethan. I can remember having that feeling, Lizzie thought—like about six minutes ago!

"Oh, who am I kidding?" Andie said miserably. "He'll never notice me. I'm just a sevie." Her voice dragged on the word as though it were a curse.

Lizzie scoffed. "You're more than 'just a sevie,'" she assured her new friend. "Okay, everything may seem a little confusing right now, but don't worry—I'll help you out." She smiled confidently.

"Wow, Lizzie," Andie said thankfully. "I'll never be like you. You're so . . . together."

Lizzie giggled. If Andie only knew how *not* together I used to be, Lizzie thought, she'd fall down laughing.

"And I'm so . . . not," Andie finished. She looked dejected.

i really like this girl.

"Oh, I know it may seem that way, but if it weren't for my friends last year, I would have never survived," Lizzie admitted.

"And I don't know how I'd survive without you," Andie said, brightening.

Have i mentioned how much i like this girl?

Look at how well my good deed is going,

Lizzie thought, giving herself a silent pat on the back.

"You're so smart," Andie went on, "really friendly . . . we even like the same boy. You know what? You're more than a friend." Andie lifted her chin and said confidently, "You're my role model."

i *love* this girl!

Lizzie had to stop herself from giving Andie a hug. After all—role models were supposed to act poised. Weren't they? Actually, Lizzie had no idea. She'd never been a role model before.

And she couldn't wait to start!

CHAPTER TWO

When Mr. and Mrs. McGuire got home from grocery shopping that afternoon, they immediately noticed an addition to their kitchen: namely, Matt. He was lying still and silent on the kitchen table with his Wilderness Cadets hat over his face.

"Matt, honey," Mrs. McGuire asked as she leaned over her son, "is something wrong?"

"I'm depressed," Matt said, his voice muffled beneath his hat.

"Depressed?" Mr. McGuire echoed. "You're too young to be depressed. What's the matter?"

Matt pulled his hat off his face. "Wilderness Cadets," he said unhappily.

Mrs. McGuire frowned. "But you love Wilderness Cadets," she protested. "What's wrong?"

"Well, you know how we earn patches for stuff?" Matt said. "Like when we read stories to old people, clean up a playground, or wash Dad's car . . ."

"You have them wash your car?" Mrs. McGuire asked her husband.

Mr. McGuire flashed his wife a guilty look.

"But if I don't earn at least one patch of my own," Matt went on, "they're going to demote me to . . ." Matt put the hat back over his head. "Bunny Cadets," he wailed, imagining himself in some sort of humiliating Bunny uniform, complete with a perky rabbit-eared hat.

The mental picture alone made him shudder.

Mr. McGuire dropped the groceries on the table. This was bad news.

"I'm sure you could get a patch in ugly," Lizzie suggested as she strode into the kitchen and yanked open the fridge.

"I'm sure I could," Matt said.

"Did you just agree with an insult?" Lizzie asked, just as Matt said, "Did I just agree with an insult?" Matt sat up and stared straight ahead, stunned.

"Wow, he really is depressed," Mr. McGuire said.

"So, what's this Bunny Cadets, anyway?" Lizzie asked.

"I'll tell you. Do you know what they do in Bunny Cadets?" Matt asked. "They take naps. Finger-paint. Make ceramic handprints." He shuddered and shook his head. Bunny Cadets was for little kids. If he had to join, it would

be the most humiliating experience of his life.

"Well, there is no way you are going to have to go back to Bunny Cadets," Mrs. McGuire said firmly.

"Well, if I don't earn a patch of my own by this weekend," Matt said, scowling at his parents, "I'm quitting."

"No, you're not," Mr. McGuire insisted. "You're not a quitter."

"No," Lizzie piped up, "apparently, he's a bunny." She smiled smugly.

"Lizzie!" Mrs. McGuire said sternly. Then she turned to her unhappy son. "Matt, your father and I are going to help you earn a patch of your own, no matter what it takes. Okay? Right, Sam?" She looked to her husband.

"Yeah, yeah," Mr. McGuire said quickly. "It'll be fun."

Matt just groaned and flopped back onto

the table. He was going to end up a Bunny Cadet. He just knew it.

"*Bonjour*, Lizzie," Miranda said as she strode toward Lizzie's open locker door. "*Comment ça va?*" A dark-haired girl slammed the locker shut and faced Miranda. "You're not Lizzie," Miranda said with a frown. So what are you doing at her locker? thought Miranda.

"No, I'm Andie," the seventh grader said brightly. "But I'm flattered by your mistake. You must be Miranda."

"You're the sevie, aren't you?" Miranda asked suspiciously as she and Andie fell into step down the hall. She noticed that Andie had changed her hairstyle. It was curlier, and she wore a thin, sparkly headband. It was a cool look.

"Lizzie's told me all about you," Andie gushed.

"She has?" Miranda frowned. "Wait, why are you stalking her locker?" Frankly, Miranda was amazed that Andie had even been able to get the thing open. Lizzie always seemed to have some kind of trouble with the lock, the door, or both.

"I was organizing it," Andie explained. "Her sosh class just finished, so she'll need her bio book next."

Miranda blinked in surprise. "You arranged her books in class order?"

"It's the least I can do," Andie said, "she's been so great to me. Like I told her, she's a great role model."

Miranda's jaw dropped.

"Hey," Lizzie said as she and Gordo walked out of their sociology class.

Miranda grabbed Lizzie's arm and nodded at Andie. "Where'd you find her and how can I get one?" she demanded.

Lizzie laughed. "Andie, your hair looks so cute like that," she said, noticing Andie's new hairstyle.

"You like it?" Andie touched her waves self-consciously. "I kind of copied what you did yesterday," she admitted.

"Look, I'm just going to cut to the chase," Gordo said to Andie. "I really think that you should stop copying other people and forge your own path."

"You're Gordo, aren't you?" Andie asked.

Gordo cocked an eyebrow.

"You'll have to excuse him," Miranda said quickly. "He's socially challenged." She gave Andie a bright smile. "So . . . do you have any friends who are looking for a role model? 'Cause I'm available."

"It's just, I'm such a fan of your work," Andie said to Gordo.

"My work?" Gordo repeated.

"That video you made last year?" Andie prompted. "Where everyone revealed their deepest thoughts about school?" Andie sighed and gazed up at the ceiling. "It's one of my all-time favorite student films," she said sincerely.

Gordo looked dumbfounded. "Really?"

Lizzie frowned slightly.

Um, hello? i thought you were the president of *my* fan club.

Andie glanced at her watch. "Ooh, look at the time," she said. She turned to Lizzie, smiled disarmingly, and chirped. "As Lizzie once said to me, tardiness is laziness."

Lizzie smiled back.

That's better.

"It was really nice meeting you both," Andie said to Miranda and Gordo. "Oh, and, Lizzie, I took your advice on Mr. Pettus's class. If you sit toward the back, you really *don't* get drenched by his talk spittle." She shook her head as though Lizzie were the Fountain of All Knowledge.

Miranda and Gordo nodded, knowingly. They had learned that lesson the hard way.

Andie smiled hugely and gave them a little wave. "Later."

"See you on the flip side," Lizzie called as her seventh-grade friend hurried down the hall.

Miranda stared after Andie as though she were the world's greatest surprise present. "I want someone to arrange my locker," she said eagerly. "And wear her hair like me. *I* want to be someone's role model!" Miranda was so

excited, she was practically bouncing up and down.

Gordo shook his head. "She's amazing."

i hate to say it, but i'll say it.

Lizzie gave a smug little shrug. "I told you, Gordo."

Who am i kidding? i love to say it!

Look at how well this good deed is going! Lizzie thought as she watched Andie walk down the hall. Soon, every sevie will have an eighth-grade role model—and it will all be thanks to me!

CHAPTER THREE

Matt walked out onto the back patio, reading his Wilderness Cadets handbook. "It says here that I can earn my nature patch by collecting and identifying leaves," he told his dad, who was sitting on a wicker love seat next to a bag of leaves. He and Matt had raked them up this morning as Part One of Operation Anti-Bunny.

"Okay, leaf number one," Mr. McGuire said as he pulled a specimen out of the bag.

He held it up, then sniffed it to see if it had any identifying odors.

"Let me see if I can find it in the book," Matt said as he flipped through the pages. "No . . . no . . ." He ran his finger across the pictures.

Mr. McGuire scratched his arm.

"No . . ."

"Here, let me see," Mr. McGuire said as he pulled the book away from Matt. "Okay." He held up the leaf so that he could compare it to the photos in the handbook. "'Pointed leaves . . . cluster of three . . .'" Mr. McGuire scratched his nose, then his neck.

"Hey!" Matt said suddenly, noticing the blotches appearing on his dad's arms and neck. "Why are you all red?"

"Huh? Where?" Mr. McGuire asked, scratching his arm.

"On your hands and your arms, and—"

Matt looked at his dad's face and grimaced. "Ew, look at your nose!" he cried.

"What?" Mr. McGuire asked, alarmed. "What about my nose?" He was scratching like crazy now.

"It's disgusting. It's all red and blotchy," Matt said.

"It is?" Mr. McGuire scratched his neck and chest some more. He still had the leaf in his hand. In fact, he was using it to do some of the scratching.

"And why are you scratching?" Matt asked.

"I don't know," Mr. McGuire said. "I'm just—I'm all itchy." He gave the handbook back to Matt so that he could scratch himself better.

"Um, Dad?" Matt said as he looked through the book, then at the leaf.

"Yeah?" Mr. McGuire asked distractedly.

"I identified the leaf," Matt said.

"Well, that's good, son, because now you'll

get your Wilderness patch." Mr. McGuire stood up. Even his back was itching now.

Matt looked up at his dad. "Unfortunately, poisonous leaves don't count."

"Uh . . . poisonous leaves?" Mr. McGuire asked slowly.

Matt nodded at the leaf in his father's hand. "That's poison ivy." He held out the book so that his dad could see the picture.

"Poison ivy?" Mr. McGuire repeated. He lifted his leg to scratch his shin and lost his balance. His arms windmilled wildly, but it didn't help. He tripped over a garden gnome and fell off the deck.

"Let's see," Matt said calmly as he flipped through the Wilderness Cadets handbook. "First aid. Ice required." He looked at his father, who was lying facedown on the lawn. "Should I get the ice?" Matt asked.

Mr. McGuire spat a chunk of grass out of

his mouth. "Yeah," he said as he rolled over onto his back. "And, uh, maybe some calamine lotion. Ow." He grabbed his ankle. "I think there's a crutch in the hall closet."

Matt gave his dad a salute and turned toward the kitchen. He took one step, then stopped and turned back. "Oh, and is the ambulance necessary or not?" he called.

"Not this time, son," Mr. McGuire said.

"Okay." Matt frowned. "Are you sure, or should I call Mom?"

"Just go!" Mr. McGuire cried. He shook his head as Matt hurried off. So far, helping his son earn this patch wasn't as much fun as he had hoped it would be.

Lizzie walked into the Digital Bean, wearing her favorite tiger-print T-shirt and black pants. She, Gordo, and Miranda had a date to study together at the cybercafé, and Lizzie

could hardly wait to see her friends and catch up. After all, it had been almost two hours since they'd hung out! There was a lot to talk about.

"Hey, Andie," a guy said as Lizzie walked into the café.

Lizzie frowned. Huh? That was kind of weird. Someone thought she was Andie.

The Digital Bean busboy smiled at her as he passed by. "Good to see you again, Andie."

Whoa. Lizzie stopped. Something was definitely up.

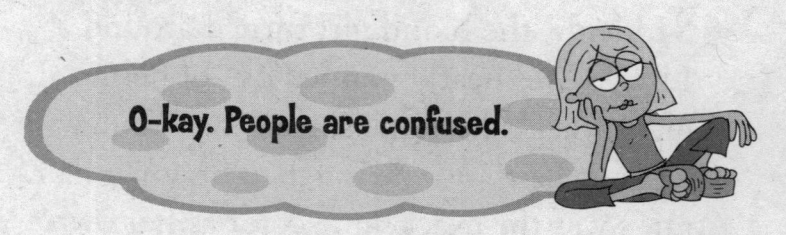

O-kay. People are confused.

Lizzie spotted Gordo and Miranda nearby, chatting with a girl who had wavy blond hair. Lizzie stopped in her tracks. She stared at the

girl's outfit, then down at her own: tiger-print T-shirt and black pants. They were dressed exactly the same!

Hey! Who is that, and why is she wearing my clothes?

"Oh, hey, Lizzie, over here!" Miranda waved Lizzie over.

Suddenly, the blond girl turned around.

Lizzie's eyes nearly popped out of her head. "Uh, Andie!" she said, surprised. "You, you dyed your hair?" Lizzie touched her own hair. Andie's was the exact same color as her own!

"Oh, good, you're here," Andie said with a big smile. She held out a tall drink topped with whipped cream. "Your smoothie is melting."

"Thanks," Lizzie said as she stared at the drink. She really didn't want it. All Lizzie wanted to know was why she suddenly had a clone. "But I—"

"I thought you could use an afternoon pick-me-up," Andie explained, cutting Lizzie off. "I know it's your favorite." She glanced over at Miranda gratefully and grinned. "Miranda told me."

Gordo and Miranda smiled at each other.

"Andie," Lizzie said, "you're dressed exactly like me."

"Isn't it great?" Gordo said enthusiastically, adjusting the straps on his backpack.

Lizzie glared at him.

impostor! What have you done with my Gordo?

"Oh," Andie said, "and before I forget, here are some flash cards to help you study for your English test." Andie smiled innocently and passed Lizzie a packet of hand-labeled cards.

"How'd you know I had a test?" Lizzie asked. She was grateful for Andie's help, but—honestly—this was getting a little irritating.

Andie shrugged, not bothering to explain, but Lizzie was sure she noticed Gordo giving Miranda a guilty look. *Hmmmmm.*

"'Kay, guys. We're outie," Andie said over her shoulder to Gordo and Miranda. "The mall is waiting." She gave her new blond hair a toss. "See you on the flip side, Lizzie."

See you on the flip side? Lizzie thought as she watched her friends begin to follow Andie out of the café. That's *my* line, thought Lizzie, and those are *my* friends!

"Miranda!" Lizzie cried.

"What?" Miranda asked defensively. "Some of her friends are going to the mall. They may need me." She glanced at the flash cards in Lizzie's hand. "Plus, you have that test to study for. Later." She waved and hurried after Andie.

Lizzie didn't know what to say. "I cannot believe her!" she complained as Gordo walked up to her.

"I know," Gordo said absently. He took a deep breath. "See you later."

"Gordo?" Lizzie called pleadingly.

"Look," Gordo said patiently, "I know how I said that Andie should forge her own path . . ."

Lizzie nodded expectantly.

". . . but you're helping to mold her," Gordo went on. "It's working. She's really cool." He sounded seriously impressed.

"Don't you mean *I'm* cool?" Lizzie asked.

"What can I say?" Gordo replied. "She wears you well. Truth is, if she wasn't a sevie, I'd probably ask her out." He waggled his eyebrows.

Lizzie curled her lip in disgust. "What?" she asked. "Well, you might as well ask *me* out."

Gordo looked freaked. "Why would I want to do that?"

Lizzie narrowed her eyes at him. "Never mind, okay?" She gestured after Andie. "She is dressing exactly like me. Am I the only one who's completely creeped out by this?"

"Yeah," Gordo said. "Gotta go," he added quickly. "Andie's waiting." He spun on his heel and walked off.

"Gordo?" Lizzie called again. But this time he didn't answer. He just kept walking.

I can't believe this! Lizzie thought. I'm left

here alone with a bunch of flash cards and a melted smoothie in a café where everyone thinks my name is Andie! What is wrong with this picture?

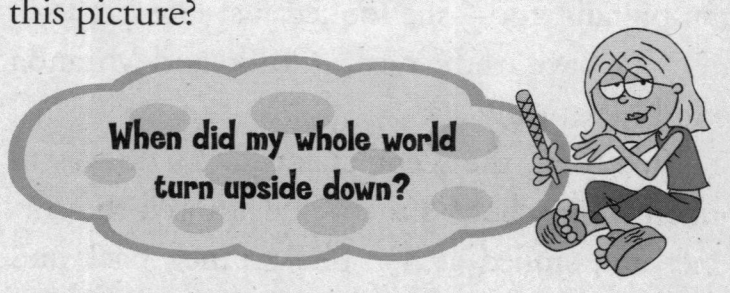

When did my whole world turn upside down?

Lizzie sighed. When did this good deed go so bad?

That night, Lizzie had trouble sleeping. She was tossing and turning, lost in a horrible nightmare.

"Lizzie, is that you?" Gordo asked as Lizzie walked toward him, wearing a pink tank top and her hair in pigtails. His voice was a ghostly echo.

"'Cause we don't need you anymore,"

Miranda said, giving her a creepy grin.

Suddenly, Andie appeared in the same pink tank top that Lizzie was wearing. Her hair was in pigtails, too—she looked just like Lizzie!

"We have Andie now," Gordo and Miranda said robotically.

Just then, the scene changed. Lizzie was in the hall at school. Ethan Craft turned the corner and smiled at her. She grinned back and fiddled with her hair. He's going to come say "Hi," Lizzie thought.

Ethan gave a double-finger-pistol "hey there" gesture, just as a blond girl walked up to him. His eyes lit up, and he put his arm around her shoulder. When the girl turned around, Lizzie saw who it was—Andie. The girl gave Lizzie a tight little superior smile and then walked off with Ethan!

The scene changed again. Lizzie saw her family eating dinner at the kitchen table. But

someone was in her place, wearing the exact same maroon long-sleeved jersey she was. Lizzie felt like she was outside herself, watching herself. Suddenly, the girl at the table turned around. That was when Lizzie realized she wasn't watching herself at all. She was watching Andie!

"Hi, Lizzie," Andie said in a syrupy voice. "You're my role model . . . role model . . . role model . . . role model . . . role model . . . role model . . . role model . . . role model. . . ."

As the words echoed through the nightmare, Lizzie put her hands over her ears. She couldn't take it anymore!

Just then, she woke up. What a horrible dream! But it couldn't have been real—could it have been?

Lizzie crept out of bed and walked to the mirror. She just wanted to make sure that she was still herself. But when she looked in

the mirror, the face that grinned back at her was—Andie's!

Lizzie screamed—and that was when she really *did* wake up. Gasping for air, Lizzie knew she'd just had the most frightening nightmare of her life. And the worst part was—it was practically coming true! She had to put a stop to this seventh-grade robot-girl she'd created . . . and she had to do it soon.

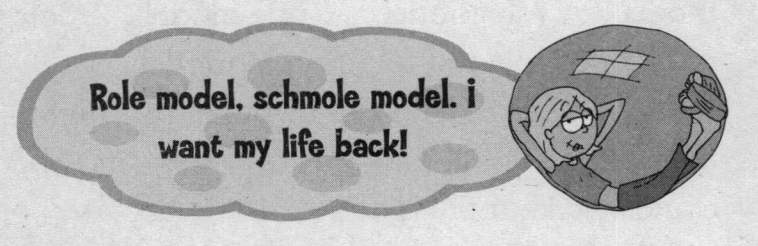

Role model, schmole model. i want my life back!

* * *

"Okay," Mr. McGuire said as he hobbled to the edge of the deck on a pair of crutches. He had set up a makeshift hearth, over which hung a blue pot. "Survival cooking," he said

confidently, naming the new patch he and Matt were trying for. "This'll be easy." Mr. McGuire bent to rub a stick against a rough rock under the pot.

"I like the way you think, Dad," Matt said unenthusiastically as he banged a rock against a can of beans. "So, how's the fire coming?"

"Good," Mr. McGuire said heartily, even though there wasn't the faintest trace of a spark coming from his stick. "How's it going with you?"

"Good. Good," Matt lied, eyeing his can of beans. The top was now completely smashed in, but the can showed no sign of coming open.

Mr. McGuire decided he needed something to help his fire along. He tossed a handful of leaves next to his stick and blew on them gently as he continued to rub the twig against the rock. "Hey!" he cried as a thin

stream of smoke began to trickle from the leaves. "It's working!" Mr. McGuire shouted excitedly. He blew on the leaves and rubbed even harder. Suddenly, the leaves burst into flame.

"Should I get the ice, Dad?" Matt asked, wincing at the sight of his father's singed eyebrows.

"Yup," Mr. McGuire replied.

CHAPTER FOUR

"But I thought you liked being Andie's role model," Miranda protested as she, Gordo, and Lizzie headed down the hall the next day.

"I'm not her role model," Lizzie snapped. "She's *imitating* me." Honestly, Lizzie thought, I know Miranda wants to be someone's role model, but can't she take my side in this? She's supposed to be my friend—and she hardly knows Andie!

"Well, you know what they say: imitation is the sincerest form of flattery," Gordo said.

Lizzie had to bite back a groan. Leave it to Gordo to come up with a cliché at a time like this! "Gordo," Lizzie said impatiently, "she dyed her hair exactly like me and she dresses exactly like me, too!" This is beyond imitation, Lizzie thought—it's a freaky impersonation!

And it's freaking me out!

"So, what are you going to do?" Miranda asked.

Lizzie sighed. "Well, I still want to set a good example. So, I'm going to let her down easy."

"Let her down easy?" Gordo demanded. His voice was borderline hysterical. "Let her down easy?" He held up his hands in a pleading gesture. "Lizzie, I beg you—please think before you do this."

Lizzie stared at him. "You really are begging

me," she said. "And it's kind of creeping me out."

"Don't get me wrong," Gordo said. "I mean, having one Lizzie is great. But if there were two of you"—he looked up at the sky as though trying to find the right description of what would happen—"words just couldn't describe it."

Lizzie rolled her eyes.

Miranda put her hand to her chest and breathed a sigh of relief. "Good."

Lizzie nodded knowingly. Some of Gordo's descriptions could get a little out of control. Especially when he brought out the megaton vocab.

"Okay, here she comes," Lizzie said quickly as she spotted Andie. It wasn't that hard. The sevie was wearing the exact same outfit Lizzie had on—a pair of red pants and a black cartoon-printed jersey. Lizzie felt like she was watching a mirror walk toward her. If I had

spinach caught in my teeth, Lizzie wondered, would Andie want to add some, too?

"Look at her outfit," Miranda said admiringly. "She's got such style."

Lizzie huffed and looked down at her own clothes. "Don't you mean *my* outfit?"

Miranda's eyebrows rose in surprise, as though she had just noticed Lizzie's clothes, and she gave her a "looking good" signal.

Lizzie snorted. The worst thing about having a seventh-grade clone was that people seemed to think that Andie made a better Lizzie than Lizzie!

"Hi, you guys," Andie burbled as she hurried over. "Guess what, Lizzie? I changed my schedule to match yours." Andie giggled. "I thought it'd be easier to pick your brain between classes that way."

"She's so smart." Gordo shook his head in awe.

"Look, Andie," Lizzie said as she drew her seventh-grade friend aside, "that's really sweet of you, but, I think that, uh . . ." She gestured from herself to Andie. "I think that we should try to create some space between us."

"Space?" Andie smiled uncertainly. "What do you mean?"

You know—space! Like the distance between here and Pluto!

Clearly, the subtle approach was not working, Lizzie thought. I'm going to have to take the direct route. Robo-girl has got to go.

"Okay, look," Lizzie tried again. "I'm really glad to be here for you to give you counsel and guidance and everything, you know? But I really, really think you need to focus a little more on *you*, and a little less on *me*."

Gordo gasped in horror.

"That's our cue, Gordo," Miranda said as she rushed over to Andie. "But if you ever need a—"

Lizzie pushed Miranda aside before she could get caught in Robo-girl's trap again. Lizzie definitely didn't want Andie to become a Miranda clone. After all, *one* Miranda was already more than enough for Lizzie to handle. Luckily, Miranda took the hint. She grabbed Gordo's hand and scurried off.

"Did I do something wrong?" Andie asked Lizzie. Tears welled up in her eyes.

Lizzie felt kind of bad, but she knew that she had to stay strong. She just couldn't let Andie take over her life! "Okay." Lizzie bit her lip. "How can I say this?"

Get lost! Get your own life! Get real and deal!

"Oh, I get it," Andie said suddenly, understanding dawning over her face.

"You do?" Lizzie asked, relieved. Whew, she thought. Thank goodness I didn't have to get too harsh with her. "Oh, good," she said. "I knew you'd understand."

Andie giggled. "You are so sweet."

Lizzie frowned in confusion. Okay—not the response I was expecting, she thought. "I am?" Lizzie asked.

"Lizzie, Lizzie, Lizzie." Andie rolled her eyes and shook her head. "If this is about me and Ethan, there's no question." She reached out and squeezed Lizzie's arm. "You saw him first; he's all yours." She smiled, as though that settled everything.

"Wh-wh-what?" Lizzie gasped.

Okay, go directly to freak—do not stop at normal.

"Ooh, there's the bell," Andie said perkily. "I want to get a good seat in math to avoid sitting next to someone who'll cheat off my paper and land me in detention." She winked at Lizzie. "Another great lesson from Lizzie history. Bye!"

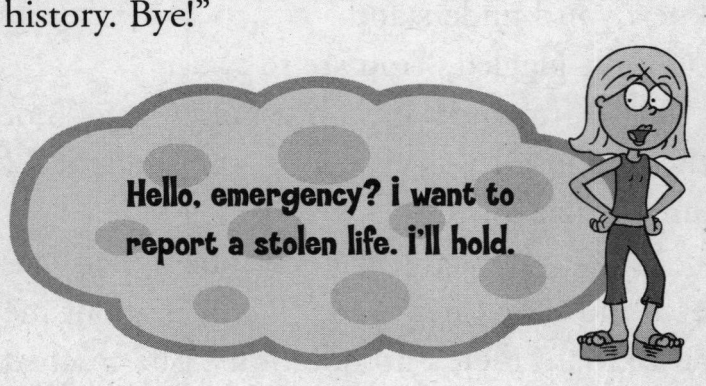

Hello, emergency? i want to report a stolen life. i'll hold.

Lizzie just stood there, too stunned to move. What had just happened? Whatever it was, it was definitely one for the ex-files. As in, ex-tremely bizarre.

Seventh graders could be so strange.

CHAPTER FIVE

"The flowers are so easy to do, too," Miranda said, holding out her manicure for Lizzie to inspect. "Andie showed me."

"That's because *I* showed her!" Lizzie huffed as they walked in the McGuires' back door.

Suddenly, Lizzie froze. "Miranda, look!" Lizzie said, gasping. Robo-girl was right there, in her very own hallway! "What's Andie doing here?" Lizzie whispered. "In my house? Talking to my mom?" Even worse, Gordo was

standing right beside her, his hands in his pockets, as though everything was perfectly normal.

"Oh, good," Miranda said, ignoring Lizzie. Then she gestured to Andie and said, "We're supposed to trade CDs. Her collection's amazing!"

Lizzie let out a sigh of frustration.

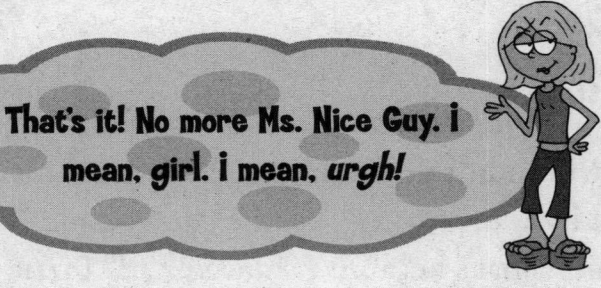

That's it! No more Ms. Nice Guy. I mean, girl. I mean, *urgh!*

"Thanks for the recipe, Mrs. McGuire," Andie said in her most sugary, oversweetened, aspartame-flavored voice. She sighed with pleasure as Mrs. McGuire handed her a recipe card. "Oven-fried chicken is my favorite."

Mrs. McGuire smiled. "That's funny—it's

Lizzie's, too," she said, clearly eating up Andie's whole nice-girl routine.

"Me, too," Gordo chimed in, looking eagerly at Andie.

Just then, Matt walked through the hall. "Freak," he said automatically as he brushed past the Lizzie clone.

"Dweeb," Andie replied.

"Gnat," Matt said without looking back.

"Rat," Andie said.

Suddenly, Matt realized the truth. He stopped in his tracks and let out a scream. "Who are you?" he demanded, horrified, as he turned around. "And please tell me you're not staying," he begged. "*One* Lizzie's bad enough!"

"Matt," Mrs. McGuire scolded, "that is no way to talk to your sister's friend."

"She's not my friend," Lizzie said, stepping into the hallway. Her arms were crossed, and she was frowning.

"Lizzie!" Mrs. McGuire sounded shocked.

Matt gazed in panic from Lizzie to her clone, then back again.

"Hey, Lizzie," Andie said cheerily. "I came by just to make sure we were okay." She made a sympathetic face, then added gently, "Things felt a little tense between us at school today."

Tense? Tense? i'll give you tense!

Robo-girl, Lizzie thought, you are going to be *past* tense when I'm done with you!

"What are you doing here?" Lizzie demanded and then held up her hand. "Don't answer that, okay? Just leave me alone! Stop dressing like me, stop doing your hair like me, and stop talking like me!"

"But I want to be like you," Andie said.

Her voice sounded hurt. "You're my role model."

"No, I'm not!" Lizzie shouted.

"Yes, you are!" Gordo pointed out.

Lizzie narrowed her eyes at Gordo until they were tiny slits. Then she turned back to Andie and sighed. "You don't want to be like me, trust me."

"She's right, you know," Matt piped up.

Mrs. McGuire gave him a warning look.

"I oversleep," Lizzie went on, "I get stains on my clothes; I trip in the cafeteria; I lose my keys; my room is a mess . . ." Lizzie pressed her lips together and shook her head. "And I try really, really hard to make my life look easy."

"Okay, maybe she went a little too far," Miranda admitted, motioning in Andie's direction, "but you have to admit," she said to Lizzie, "your locker looks awesome."

"Okay, let's focus on the 'too far' part," Lizzie said, exasperated. Then she turned back to Andie. "Do you get it now?" she asked gently.

Gordo shook his head. "Not really."

Andie stood there a moment. "Sorry I bothered you," she said finally. Her voice sounded strangled. Andie didn't look back as she ran out the front door.

Mrs. McGuire and Gordo stared at Lizzie with disappointment. Then Gordo sighed and looked at the floor.

"Honey, what was that all about?" Mrs. McGuire asked quietly.

"Andie was taking over my life, Mom," Lizzie explained. "She left me no choice."

"You know," Matt put in, rubbing his chin, "you forgot to say that you snore, that you leave your hair in the brush, and that your toes stick together when it's hot out."

"They do?" asked Miranda.

Lizzie groaned. Okay, maybe describing her flaws hadn't been the greatest idea. No doubt, Matt would use it against her for the rest of her life.

But if it had gotten rid of Robo-girl, it was definitely worth it.

"Mom, I've made a decision," Matt said as he sat down on his bed next to his mother later that evening. "I'm quitting Wilderness Cadets."

"Oh, honey," Mrs. McGuire said, wrapping him in a hug. "You're just having trouble earning your patches, that's all."

"Hey, honey?" Mr. McGuire asked as he hobbled into Matt's room. His arms were bandaged where the leaf fire had gotten out of control, but at least his eyebrows were back to normal. "Have we got any more calamine lotion?" he asked.

"I'll get it, Dad," Matt volunteered, "and

you really should be sitting down." Matt dragged the rolling chair out from behind his desk and gestured for his father to take it.

"You're probably right, son," Mr. McGuire said as he struggled into the chair. "Good thinking."

"And we need to elevate your leg," Matt added as he propped his father's sprained ankle onto his bed.

"Oh, that's a great idea," Mr. McGuire said. He leaned back comfortably.

Mrs. McGuire stood up to make room for her husband's foot on the bed. She picked up Matt's Wilderness Cadets handbook and started flipping through it.

"And you're going to scar if you keep scratching like that!" Matt scolded as Mr. McGuire reached for his neck.

"Boy, Matt," Mrs. McGuire said, "you sure know your first-aid stuff." Still flipping

through the handbook, she sat down on the bed. Unfortunately, she sat down on Mr. McGuire's ankle, too.

"Ow!" Mr. McGuire cried.

"I'm sorry!" Mrs. McGuire apologized as she pulled her husband's foot into her lap.

"It's basic Wilderness Cadets training," Matt said with a shrug. "It's all in the manual."

"Well, honey, you don't have to quit Cadets," Mrs. McGuire said as she pointed to something in the handbook.

"I don't?" Matt asked. He peered at the section his mom had found.

"No. You just earned your first-aid patch!" She leaped off the bed and pulled Matt into a huge bear hug. "Congratulations, sweetie."

"Um . . . guys . . ." Mr. McGuire called. When Mrs. McGuire had jumped up, she had knocked his foot aside, and now he was rolling backward out the door.

"Oh, I'm so proud of you," Mrs. McGuire gushed, not noticing her husband.

"Um . . . guys . . ." Mr. McGuire shouted, more loudly this time. His chair was rolling down the hall!

Mrs. McGuire and Matt ran to help him, but it was too late—Mr. McGuire was out of control and headed for the stairs! "Ugh-ugh-ugh-ugh-ugh," he grunted as he bounced down every step. Finally, the chair landed at the bottom, and Mr. McGuire spilled facedown onto the entranceway carpet.

Mrs. McGuire and Matt winced.

"Ice, Dad?" Matt suggested.

"Yup," Mr. McGuire said wearily.

That first-aid patch was really coming in handy.

"I still feel kind of bad about the way things ended with Andie," Lizzie confessed to

Miranda and Gordo the next day in school. Gordo had finally forgiven her for hurting Andie's feelings, and Miranda had finally given up on becoming someone's role model. Things are finally back to normal, Lizzie thought, even though I hate that I had to be mean to Andie to make them that way.

"Uh-oh," Miranda warned. "Kate and posse approaching."

Lizzie groaned.

"Just when I thought I was having a good day," Gordo said.

"You guys, that's Kate and *Andie*!" Miranda said as the group of popular girls strutted down the hallway.

Lizzie's jaw dropped. Kate and Andie were both wearing pastel-pink sweaters with feathers at the cuffs, and they both had fluffy pink hair holders in their frosted blond hair. Andie had gone from being a Lizzie-clone to being a

Kate-clone. "She's got hair extensions!" Lizzie was in shock.

"Hello, Lizzie McGuire," Kate said snidely.

"Hello, Lizzie McGuire," Andie said just as snidely.

The sight was so ridiculous, it actually made Lizzie laugh.

"I just thought I should let you know," Kate went on, "everyone thought I'm a much better role model than you."

"Way better," Andie agreed. "Kate's got, like, shopping tips, and hair and makeup advice." She looked Lizzie up and down. "You know, really important stuff," she sneered.

Lizzie put her hand to her cheek. "How will I go on?" Lizzie asked dramatically.

Kate held up her fingers in a giant *W*. "Whatever," she said. "You live and learn, right, Andie?"

"That's what I always say," Andie replied.

She hesitated a minute. "Isn't it?" she asked in a low voice. Kate nodded, and Andie smiled. "Live and learn," Andie parroted.

"Hi, Andie," Gordo said, giving the seventh grader a friendly wave.

"Later." Kate and Andie held up their hands in an identical gesture, and then they strutted off down the hall.

Gordo frowned. "Well," he said to Lizzie, "if it makes you feel any better, you were a way better role model than Kate."

"That's a given," Miranda agreed, "Although," she added thoughtfully, "I did like the lip gloss they were wearing."

"Well, you know, it shouldn't be about the lip gloss," Lizzie said. "Andie should want to copy someone, you know, for the important stuff, like being a better person."

Miranda nodded. "Maybe being a role model is harder than I thought. Plus," she

added with a grin, "it's more fun to find things out on your own."

"Well, we've all done okay," Lizzie said.

"And you never figure out who you really are if you're busy trying to be someone else," Gordo said.

"Oh, Gordo's back!" Lizzie said excitedly as she leaned in and gave him a hug.

"Yeah," Gordo said, ducking away from the public display of affection. "I liked two Lizzies," he admitted, "but two Kates? That's scary." He shuddered.

Lizzie laughed. Too true.

She was glad that there was only one of her. And that her two best friends had finally seen the light. Let the fem-clones hang out together, Lizzie thought as she smiled at Gordo and Miranda. I've got everyone I need right here.

* * *

Don't close the book on Lizzie yet!
Here's a sneak peek at the next
Lizzie McGuire story. . . ."

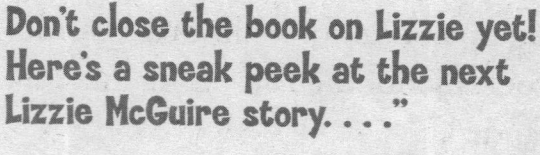

Adapted by Jasmine Jones

Based on the television series, "Lizzie McGuire", created by Terri Minsky

Based on a teleplay written by Nina G. Bargiel & Jeremy J. Bargiel

"Pudding cup!" Gordo called. He was standing on a table in the middle of the crowded lunch patio, holding his dessert over his head. "Sealed! Untouched by cafeteria-lady hands! No skin! Do I hear one dollar?" A kid at a nearby table lifted his spoon in the air. "I've got a dollar. Do I hear one twenty-five?"

Lizzie and Miranda walked over to Gordo's table, carrying their lunch trays. They stood there, staring up at him for a minute. "Gordo, why are you auctioning off your lunch?" Lizzie demanded.

"I need to make money for a new stereo," Gordo explained.

Miranda scrunched up her face and glanced at Lizzie. The friends looked up at Gordo dubiously. He didn't step down from the table, or even lower his pudding cup.

"What about your old stereo?" Lizzie wanted to know.

"It's gone to stereo heaven," Gordo said. Suddenly, he caught a flash of movement out of the corner of his eye. "You in the striped shirt!" he called. "One-fifty for the pudding cup?" A kid in a green-yellow-and-black-striped jersey nodded and walked over. "One fifty. Going once, twice, sold! To the boy in

the striped shirt." The kid passed Gordo a fistful of change, and Gordo handed over his prized pudding cup.

"So, why don't you get your parents to buy you a new one?" Miranda asked. Lizzie guessed her friend was talking about the stereo, not the pudding cup.

"That would be the logical answer," Gordo said as he climbed down from the table. "But my parents want me to earn the money on my own."

Gordo slid into a chair, and Miranda and Lizzie plopped their trays on the table and sat down across from him.

"I hate it when they say stuff like that!" Lizzie said as she settled her mesh bag with the big flower onto the ground next to her. Seriously. Just two days before, when they were in the drugstore, Lizzie's mom had actually said that Lizzie had plenty of lip gloss,

and that if she wanted a new color, she should pay for it herself. As if lip gloss was something you could ever have "plenty" of! Parents.

"So by brown-bagging my lunch and auctioning off my desserts, I can make about three dollars a day," Gordo explained. He looked down at his juice box dejectedly. "So I'll have a new stereo in five months."

Miranda, who had just popped a fry into her mouth, stopped midchew and had to swallow fast. "Five *months?*" she asked.

Gordo nodded. "Well, if you figure three dollars a day, five days a week—that's fifteen dollars," he explained. "And there are four weeks in a month, so that would be sixty dollars."

Miranda curled her lip and thought a minute, trying to follow the math.

"So, I'll have three hundred dollars in five months," Gordo finished.

"Wow, Gordo," Lizzie said, rolling her eyes. "Where were you during the math test today?"

"I was, uh," Gordo blew on his fingernails and rubbed them against his shirt, "getting my usual A."

Miranda and Lizzie looked at each other.

Way to be modest, Gordo.

"Well, if you're so smart, Mr. A," Lizzie said, giving him another eyeball roll, "you should already know how to raise money for your new stereo."

Gordo frowned. "What are you talking about?"

"Tutor math," Lizzie said, like it was the most obvious thing in the world.

"People would totally pay for your help," Miranda chimed in.

"Oh, that's actually not a bad idea." Gordo pressed his lips together and nodded.

"Of course, it's not a bad idea." Lizzie tossed her hair and smiled. "I came up with it." She took a sip from her juice box. Besides, she thought, tutoring had to beat the humiliation of holding a daily pudding auction.

"Okay, I'll do it," Gordo said with finality. His eyes wandered over to the edge of Miranda's tray. "So, Miranda, how about a bite of that cupcake?"

Miranda picked up her cupcake and held it out toward Gordo. "Sure," she said.

Gordo grinned and reached for the cupcake, but Miranda pulled it back.

"For a buck fifty," Miranda told him with a crafty smile.

Gordo glowered at her, which only made

Lizzie laugh. So much for Gordo's brilliant moneymaking scheme!

"Hey, Gordo," Lizzie said as she and Miranda walked into English class the next afternoon, "how many people have signed up for the tutoring?" The two girls slipped into the two desks closest to Gordo, and Miranda smiled at him expectantly.

Gordo played with his pen. "Well, let's see . . . between that mad rush before school and the mob scene after first period?" He thought for a minute. "Zero."

Miranda's smile froze on her face. "Nobody's signed up yet?"

"No one," Gordo said. He dug around in his binder. "I even made these flyers."

Lizzie reached for the flyer. "Let me see that." She glanced down at the piece of paper. It looked like a chicken had crawled

over it, trying to scratch a worm out of
the paper.

How can anybody read this?
Cave paintings are easier
to understand.

Miranda grimaced at the flyer. "Is this in
English?" she asked.

Gordo frowned at her.

Lizzie's eyebrows drew together. "Who in
their right mind would respond to something
like this?"

At that very moment, Ethan—hottie of
this and every single year, past and present—
walked into class carrying a piece of paper.
"So Gor-don," he said, holding out a copy of
Gordo's flyer, "is this you?"

"Yeah," Gordo said, clearly completely

uninterested in anything Ethan had to say. Gordo glanced down at his notebook. "Yeah, it is."

Miranda's mouth fell open, and she glanced over at Lizzie. Lizzie had to press her lips together to keep from grinning like an idiot. Superhot Ethan needed a tutor! How lucky could she get? She and Miranda were practically Gordo's assistant tutors, right? After all, Lizzie had come up with the whole tutoring concept herself. They'd definitely get to hang with—er—*help* Ethan!

"So you, like, uh, tutor math and stuff, right?" Ethan asked Gordo.

"Yeah, I do." Gordo looked at the paper in Ethan's hand and shook his head, as though he couldn't believe anyone had actually had trouble understanding his gorgeous flyer.

Ethan whipped out another piece of paper. "See, I kind of flagged the last test," he

explained as he handed the exam over to Gordo, "and my 'rents think I could use some help."

Gordo frowned down at the test, like he didn't quite know what to do with it. Lizzie guessed that Mr. "A" had probably never seen a test with that much red on it before in his life.

The moment dragged on, and Lizzie's eyes bugged out. Why wasn't Gordo trying to sell himself as Ethan's tutor? Did he truly not grasp that this was a golden opportunity to hang out with the cutest guy in the known universe? Okay, it was true, Gordo was a guy. But couldn't he see what kind of an opportunity this was for Lizzie and Miranda? Lizzie snapped her fingers at Gordo. He looked up and Lizzie pointed at Ethan.

Gordo looked confused. He glanced over at Miranda, who mouthed, "Go! Go!"

Hello, Captain Obvious!

Clearly, Lizzie had to take matters into her own hands. "Oh, Ethan," Lizzie said with a nervous laugh, "Gordo could tutor you."

"Yeah, he's really smart," Miranda agreed, smiling. She turned to Gordo, and her frozen smile turned to a glare. Her glance was of the If-You-Don't-Do-This-I'll-Hurt-You variety. Lizzie knew it well.

"And we could help," Lizzie volunteered, smiling up at Ethan. "If you needed it."

"That would be cool," Ethan said. Then he turned to Gordo. "So what do you think, Profes-sor?"

Gordo stared at the test. Probably wondering whether it had gotten into a fight with a box of red pens, Lizzie guessed. "Well, I

think you could use the help," Gordo said.

"Excellent," Ethan said. He plucked the test out of Gordo's hand and headed down the row of desks. "Catch you later."

Lizzie and Miranda stared after him.

"I wish *my* stereo broke," Miranda said wistfully.

"This tutoring thing rocks, Gordo!" Lizzie said happily, looking over at Miranda. "We have a total *in* with Ethan." Lizzie and Miranda grinned at each other.

"Guys, relax," Gordo said in a bored voice. "I'm gonna be tutoring a guy who got an eleven on the test."

"That's not so bad," Miranda said.

Gordo looked at her from under heavy eyebrows. "Out of a hundred?"

Miranda grimaced and fiddled with one of the slim dark braids that stuck out from beneath her multicolored crocheted cap.

"So—he'll need lots of tutoring," Lizzie said brightly. "You'll have your stereo in no time."

Gordo glanced back at Ethan. "With the amount of tutoring this guy is going to need," he said, "I think I'll be looking at the entire home entertainment system." Gordo sighed. "With surround sound."

Lizzie giggled. She could hardly wait to hang out in front of Gordo's new home entertainment system—with Ethan by her side, of course.

Sorry! That's the end of the sneak peek for now. But don't go nuclear! To read the rest, all you have to do is look for the next title in the Lizzie McGuire series—

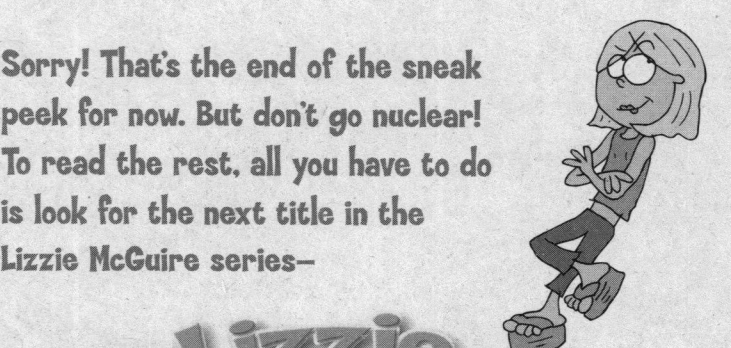

Lizzie Ethan

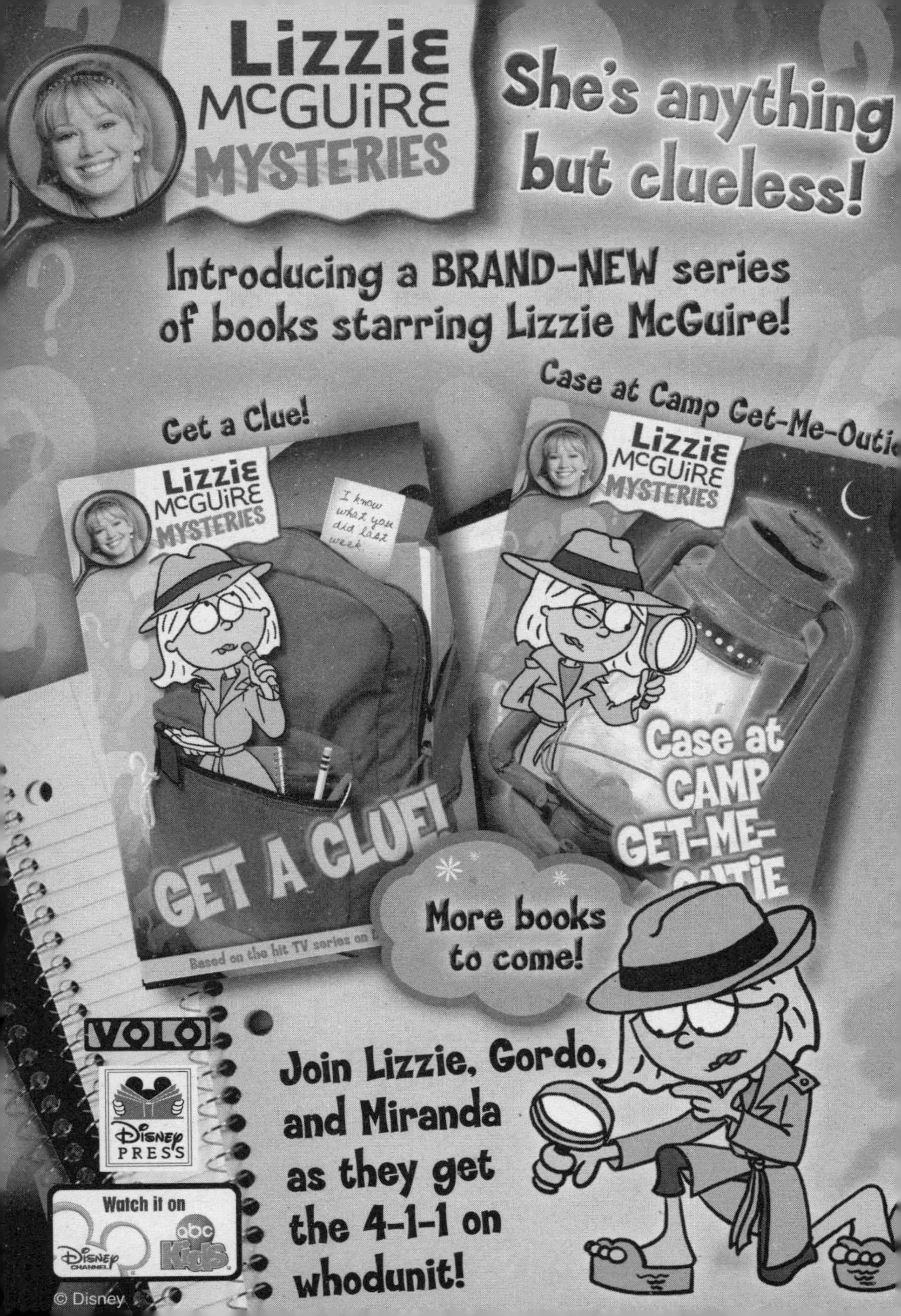

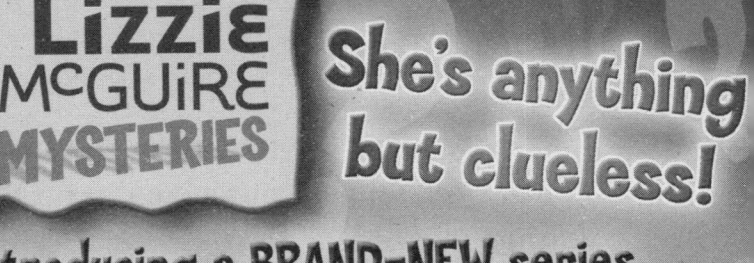